DANNY PEARSON WILL RETURN

For updates about current and upcoming releases, as well as exclusive promotions, visit the authors website at:

www.stephentaylorbooks.com

ALSO BY STEPHEN TAYLOR
THE DANNY PEARSON THRILLER SERIES

Snipe

Heavy Traffic

The Timekeepers Box

The Book Signing

Vodka Over London Ice

Execution Of Faith

Who Holds The Power

Alive Until I Die

Sport of Kings

Blood Runs Deep

Command to Kill

No Upper Limit

Leave Nothing To Chance

CHAPTER 1

'Come on, come on.' Danny Pearson muttered, crawling along in the Stratford traffic, the power of his BMW M4 totally wasted as he sat in first gear, gurgling along in the bumper-to-bumper traffic. Spotting his destination, he moved slowly forward, eyeing up a parking space ahead. A group of West Ham supporters were chanting and shouting abuse across the road at a group of Tottenham supporters who returned their taunts. Danny hung back as bottles hurtled left and right across the road in a beer- and testosterone-fuelled outburst. The situation was seconds away from escalating when a group of match day police appeared at the end of the road. The football supporters begrudgingly fell into line and continued on their way as Danny pulled into the parking space. He looked at his watch and frowned.

Shit, running late.

A little bell rang as he pushed the shop door open. Danny moved up to the counter as a man appeared from out back.

'I've got a pickup for Pearson,' he said, anxiously looking at his watch.

The man bent down and pulled a box from below the counter and placed it on the top. 'This one is yours. Careful, it's fragile.'

Danny gave him a nod, picked the box up and left. He put it on the car roof while he unlocked the passenger door. He was just about to put the box on the passenger seat when he noticed his front tyre was flat, the razor-sharp neck of a broken beer bottle protruding from underneath it.

Shit.

His phone buzzed as he pulled the flap in the boot up to get the jack and spare tyre out, only to find the tyre on the spare wheel was flat as well.

'Shit, shit,' he said, slamming the boot down and checking the message on his phone.

Have you picked it up yet? Be here by 2pm or we're both dead.

'Shit, shit, shit,' Danny said, texting back *On my way,* before grabbing the box and heading towards Stratford Tube station.

Cursing under his breath, Danny jostled through the area outside the station, taking care not to squash the box in the growing pressure cooker of police, revelling West Ham supporters and commiserating Tottenham supporters all flooding the platforms to get trains home. Looking at his watch, Danny pushed his way to the front of the platform to avoid a full train and having to wait for the next one.

'Oi, watch where you're going, grandad,' came a youthful shout from behind him.

Grandad! You cheeky bastard! he thought, entering the train without looking back.

Packed in like sardines, the doors slid shut, trapping the smell of sweat and beer in the carriage as it moved off. With his back to the crowd, Danny held the box carefully in front of him, counting the stops down as he got closer to his destination.

'Hey gorgeous, you want to come for a drink with us?' came a voice from behind him.

'No, leave me alone, please,' came a woman's dismissive response.

Don't. Not today. Just leave it, you little shit. Just leave it.

'Ah, come on, darlin', don't be like that,' said the football supporter, moving in with his mates and putting his arm around the young woman.

'Look, just fuck off will you,' she snapped back, which just made the pack laugh and jeer even more.

Oh, for fuck's sake.

Danny looked down at a grungy, pasty youth sitting in the seat beside him. His hair was long and smelled like chip fat.

'Hold this for me,' he said, telling, not asking.

Something about the intensity of Danny's look made the youth take the box without saying a word.

'Hey fellas, come on, leave the lady alone,' Danny said in his best disarming tone and smile.

'Fuck off and mind your own business, grandad,' snarled the football supporter with drunken venom, his pals closing in around him, itching to escalate the situation.

There's the grandad thing again, fucking little bastard.

'Come over here, miss. Don't worry, they won't hurt you,' Danny said, extending his hand to the young woman.

Predictably, the larger of the youths came at Danny, full of beer bravado, his arm drawing back slow and clumsy in preparation for a punch. As if watching in slow motion, Danny was already calculating several moves ahead. He dodged the punch and hammered a fist into the youths kidney. As the guy doubled-up, Danny stepped forward and kicked the supporter to the woman's left in the balls. He fell on top of his mate and slid along the floor of the train as it slowed for the next station.

'Right, pretty boy, call me grandad one more time. I dare you,' Danny said, staring menacingly at the shocked youth.

'Alright, mate, Jesus, I was only joking,' he said, backing away.

'Thank you,' the woman said, stepping past as she hurried out the door and onto the platform.

Leaving the youths to pick themselves up, Danny checked his watch, frowned, and turned to get his box.

'Oh c'mon,' he said, staring at an empty seat.

Jumping through the doors as they were shutting, Danny stood on the platform, searching the back of the crowd's heads as they left the platform. He spotted the chip fat hair of Mr Grunge as his phone buzzed with a message.

Where are you? Time's running out.

Frowning, Danny headed off in pursuit of his package, losing sight of his target now and then as he weaved in and out of the crowd. Leaving the station, he spotted Mr Grunge walking fast towards Walthamstow high street. Taking off at full pelt, Danny caught up with him, grabbing his shoulder and spun him around. The guy's eyes went wide in panic at the murderous look on Danny's face. His first thought had been to punch the little bastard out, but when he saw how pathetic he looked, Danny just grabbed the box back. Looking at his watch, he broke into a run, the phone vibrating in his pocket pushing him on even faster.

Turning off the main road, Danny headed through rows of Georgian townhouses until he saw his destination. A car pulling onto its drive caused Danny to spin behind the hedge-lined edge of the front garden and head down the alley to the rear of the house.

'Christ, where have you been?' came a voice as he ducked in through the patio doors and slid the box onto the table. The door to the kitchen opened as he lifted the lid off and chucked it under the table.

'Don't ask, bruv,' Danny answered under his breath before joining in with a happy birthday as his sister-in-law and niece entered the room.

'Look at the cake, Sophie,' said Tina, showing the two-year-old the big white cake with happy birthday and a big two on top.

'Are you alright, Danny? You're sweating like a pig,' said Tina, handing her giggling daughter to Danny's brother, Rob.

'Eh, yeah, it's nothing a nice cold beer won't fix,' said Danny, giving his niece a tickle on the way to the fridge. 'You want one, bruv?'

'Yeah, I think I need one,' Rob answered.

CHAPTER 2

On an industrial estate full of modern blue chip companies on the outskirts of Sydney, Australia, Theodore Blazer pulled his BMW i8 hybrid sports car up next to a security guard as he patrolled the car park.

'Glorious morning, Kenny,' he said, lowering the window and fixing the security man with a million-dollar smile, his blue eyes twinkling behind Ray-Ban shades.

'Certainly is, Mr Blazer. You have a good day, sir.'

'And you, Kenny,' he said cheerfully, raising the window before speeding across the car park and stopping in the CEO's parking space by the entrance door.

He got out with a spring in his step, looking like a cross between a surfer and a model in his Armani trousers and shirt undone at the top.

'Good morning, Mr Blazer,' said the woman on the reception desk, doing a poor job of hiding her adoration of him.

'Good morning, Janice. Anyone asks, I'm in a meeting

with Mr Drago in the R&D department and don't want to be disturbed.'

'Yes, Mr Blazer, of course,' she said, a little too eagerly.

'Thank you, Janice, you're a star,' Theo shouted over his shoulder, taking the stairs two at a time. After smiles and good mornings along the corridor, Theo put his hand on a panel next to the research and development department door. A green light scanned his palm before the electric door lock clicked open.

'Good morning, Bill, is Mr Drago here yet?' Theo said to the chubby security man in a little room with a desk and body scanner similar to one found in airport security.

'Yes, Mr Blazer, he came in with your two guests half an hour ago,' said Bill, sliding a little plastic tray across the desk to Theo.

'Excellent,' Theo said, dropping his phone and keys into it.

Bill slid the tray back, picked it up, and secured it in one of the small lockers behind the desk. He gave Theo a plastic disc with the number 12 on it and gestured for him to go through the scanner.

'How are the wife and kids?' Theo said, walking through the scanner without taking much notice of the light that glowed green on top of it.

He didn't need to do the security checks, but as the owner of the company, it was good for the employees to see that the rule of no photographic or electronic devices in the R&D department applied to everybody without exception.

'They're good, Mr Blazer, thank you for asking.'

'Great, keep up the good work, Bill,' Theo said, placing his hand on a second palm reader before pushing his way through the heavy fire doors into the R&D room.

The room was large and windowless, sectioned up with

workstations with an array of mounted ultra-high definition screens and keyboards and weird-shaped gaming mice, joysticks and accessories. A young woman with purple hair and large headphones nodded her head in time with the music as she typed at a blistering pace, staring at a sea of computer code on the large screen.

'Looking good, Mr B,' she said, louder than intended due to the headphones.

'Right back at ya, Nicki. Loving the purple hair this week,' Theo shouted back.

At the front of the room, the wall was full of giant monitors scrolling through different graphic designs. Above them hung a large illuminated sign with the logo of Blazer Games. Walking past it, Theo smiled at several more people before exiting out a door at the far end. In contrast to the main room, this space was bright and neat, almost clinical.

'Morning Kyle, are we ready?' asked Theo.

'Yes, they are in the games suite,' said Theo's right-hand man, Kyle Drago, his face far more serious than Theo's.

'Lighten up, Kyle, this is a great day. A lot of time and effort's gone into this, so smile.'

Kyle gave a half-hearted smile back.

'Ok, ok, forget it. You look like you're about to shit yourself. Is everyone out of this section?' said Theo, getting back to business.

'Everyone but the shrink and the test subjects,' said Kyle, ignoring Theo's teasing.

'Good, let's get on with it then,' Theo said, entering a small room with a desk, screens and computer in front of four rows of banked seating, all looking through a one-way observation window.

On the other side of the one-way glass, two young men

sat a few metres apart in matching gaming chairs, facing matching screens. A man in his late forties moved between the two of them, attaching sensors and heart monitors to a transmitter box on their chests. Each wore a stretchy hat under their headphones, full of more sensors.

'Ok, let's get this show on the road,' Theo said, fixing a smile on his face as he opened the door beside the observation window and walked through. 'Morning gentlemen, I'm Theodore Blazer, owner of Blazer Games. Thank you for participating in our little competition. I hope you have enjoyed the tour of our facility and are looking forward to taking part in our pre-production test of the additional levels for Command to Kill. Any questions?' Theo said, moving between the two to shake their hands.

'Eh, yeah, why couldn't we tell anyone about winning this and what exactly is all this stuff for?' said the youth with Andy on his visitor's badge.

'Two very good questions, Andy. The game you are about to play has been in development for five years at a cost of around seventy million dollars to make. Piracy and industrial espionage are a real threat. If our game was hacked or stolen, all that time and money would be for nothing, hence the secrecy. As for the sensors, we check heart rate, blood pressure and brain activity during play. Dr Smith here, then checks it against a database of triggers for seizures, epilepsy, migraines etcetera. We wouldn't want to release a game to find it gives fifty percent of gamers a headache, would we?'

'I guess not,' said Andy, studying the keypad.

'Ok, well, you've signed the confidentiality agreements, so let's begin. We'll back out to the observation room so you two can enjoy yourselves,' Theo said, moving out of the room after Dr Smith and Kyle.

Theo sat at the desk and typed furiously as Kyle and

the doctor sat in the tiered seating behind him. The two test subjects' screens burst into life with the Command to Kill logo. As soon as level one started they attacked the keypad vigorously, instantly engrossed in the game. Theo watched a camera image of their faces and their heart and brain activity rates rise on the monitor beside him.

'All good, Doctor?'

'They passed all the priming levels to get here. The brain activity is in the orange sector and they are fully immersed in the game. You can give them the trigger phrase any time you like,' said Dr Smith.

The tension grew as they sat silently in the little room, looking through the one-way glass. Theo slowly leaned forward and pressed the button on the microphone in front of him. 'New orders from command.'

The second he'd uttered the final word, the test subjects' pupils went wide, almost covering their irises. Their heart rates dropped and their brain activity fell into the green.

'That's it, they are under,' said the doctor.

'But they are still playing the game?' said Kyle.

'To a degree they are still conscious. If you brought them out now, they would only remember playing the game. It's like when you drive to a destination, only to realise you can't remember how you got there. Without a command, their subconscious would keep them ticking through whatever they are doing. Go ahead, give them an order.'

Theo thought for a second then pressed the mic button. 'Orders from Command: the man next to you is the enemy. Kill him, do it now.'

Both men turned and looked at each other, their eyes unreadably dark, and faces without emotion as they got up and went for each other. Being the larger and more muscular of the two, Andy's blow knocked the smaller man sideways into the games monitor, cracking the screen. Andy grabbed it as it blinked green and red, smashing it down on the other guy's head, knocking him to the ground. He punched and kicked from the floor in a futile effort to fulfil his orders, while Andy stood over him and continued to pummel him with the screen. Eventually he stopped moving and blood trickled out of his ears and nose.

'New orders from Command: stand down,' came over the speaker.

Andy dropped the screen and stood back. His pupils shrank back to normal. Shock and horror filled his face at the sight of the man's crushed head and pool of blood spreading across the light grey vinyl flooring.

'Oh Andy, what have you done?' came Theo's mock horrified voice.

'I, I don't know what happened. I was playing the game and then I'm looking at this,' stammered Andy, turning his blood covered hands over in front of him.

'Don't worry, Andy, it's going to be alright, look at me,' said Theo, moving in front of him with a reassuring smile.

As Andy looked at him with tearful eyes, he felt a sharp prick in his neck. Before he could get his hand up to investigate, the world went black and he fell to the floor, leaving the doctor standing behind him with an empty syringe in his hand.

'Excellent. The test was a complete success. Oops, must go,' Theo said, glancing at his watch. 'Excellent work Doctor. Kyle, lock this up for now. Get Maaka and his men to clean it up tonight. It's Friday, the place will be empty by six.'

CHAPTER 3

'Paul's going to freak when he gets the bill for these seats,' Danny said to his best friend Scott Miller, lounging next to him in the British Airways premium cabin pod.

'Relax, dear boy, I paid for the tickets, or rather the MacIntyre Group paid for them,' replied Scott, pressing the button for the flight attendant.

'MacIntyre Group?'

'Yes, Paul put them in touch with me after they had a rather expensive cyber attack. A group of Albanian hackers took them for a considerable amount of money. Anyway, I sorted out their woefully inadequate software, and the board insisted on flying me and my assistant— that's you by the way—all the way to Australia to kiss my backside. As a thank you to Paul for the introduction, I'm sorting out the IT for your quaint little Sydney branch of Greenwood Security,' said Scott, brushing his floppy hair back and giving the female flight attendant one of his best smiles. 'Champagne please, my dear. Daniel?'

'Eh, can I have a beer, please?'

'Certainly, sir. We do Brewdog beer if that's alright,' she replied with a smile.

'That'll be fine, thank you,' Danny said, turning back to Scott after she'd gone to get the drinks. 'So how long will you be tied up with the MacIntyre people?'

'Only for a day. They want to give me the grand tour of their offices and take me out to dinner at the famous Bennelong restaurant, that's in the Opera House in case you didn't know. That leaves me with five minutes to set up your little office and nine days to see the sights and catch up with my wayward little sister.'

'Yeah, little Nicki. Christ, last time I saw her I was leaving for basic training and she was going backpacking around the world.'

'Yes, well, she got as far as Sydney and fell in love with a bass guitarist, or was it a drummer? I can't remember. Either way, he was a total waste of space. They got married; she got citizenship. Then she caught him sleeping with one, or maybe more than one, of the groupies and swiftly got divorced. It will be nice to see her, though,' Scott smiled again as the pretty flight attendant returned with the drinks.

'She never thought of coming back to Britain?'

'No, I think the climate and the people suited her in Australia. She got a job at one of the big gaming companies, Blazer Games. She's doing quite well by all accounts. But then, she always was a gifted programmer. Just don't tell her I said that,' said Scott, lifting his drink to Danny. 'Cheers.'

'Cheers. Blazer, where have I heard the name Blazer before?'

'Well, I doubt it's from playing video games, old man. I imagine it's from Theodore Blazer's other company, Blink Defence Systems. They are responsible for a large number of military defence and government intelligence services software. I think the Pentagon and FBI use them.'

'He's worth a few quid then,' said Danny, losing interest and playing with the inflight entertainment system.

'He certainly is. I think he's up there with Mark Zuckerberg and Bill Gates on the Forbes rich list,' said Scott, slightly irritated at Danny's hammering on the touch screen in front of him.

'What?' Danny said, catching his frown.

'Press any harder and you'll punch a hole in that thing.'

'I can't get the film menu up,' said Danny, about to attack the screen again with angry fingers.

'Let me do it, you caveman. There,' Scott said, leaning across and easily moving through the menu to the film list.

'Oh, right, thanks.'

'You're welcome, dear boy. Do give me a shout if you need any further assistance. You know, with tying your shoelaces or cutting your inflight meal up,' Scott said, chuckling to himself.

'How about I open the door and drop you somewhere over the Indian Ocean?' said Danny, grinning back.

'How about we get some more drinks and order some food?' Scott said, pulling the menu card up in front of him.

'Now that sounds like a great idea. I can drop you in the Indian Ocean later.'

CHAPTER 4

Feeling good about himself, Dr Smith stopped at an off-licence on his way back to his apartment in Mattawunga, with its views of Sydney Harbour Bridge and the Opera House across the harbour. He'd been dry for over a year, ever since Theodore Blazer found him at the bottom of a bottle, drinking away his suspension for gross misconduct with a female patient. She was young and beautiful and he was awkward, geeky and unsuccessful with the ladies. His months of hypnotherapy treatment and the influence it gave him over her had been too much of a temptation for him. But today was a good day, a day that deserved a drink. He had proved everyone wrong and the project was a success. With the three million dollar bonus Blazer was going to give him, he'd move away, somewhere no one knew him, maybe New Zealand, start up a little practice and live happily ever after.

With the mental decision that he was going to have a drink made, the draw of the freshly bought whisky bottle was too great. Ducking into an alley, Dr Smith cracked the seal on the bottle and took a large gulp. He savoured the feeling for a moment, then took another swig before screwing the lid back on and continuing his walk home. Approaching his apartment block, he paused for a minute to watch the sun setting behind the city centre skyscrapers across the harbour, then entered the stairwell. Passing the second floor landing, he met a teenager from the apartment above his coming down the stairs.

'Hi, Tony.'

The boy didn't answer. He stopped in the centre of the stairs, his head down and his phone to his ear under his pulled-up hoodie.

'Excuse me,' Dr Smith said politely, moving to the side to get past.

Tony's head moved up slowly, his vacant expression coming into view, his pupils large and dark as he focused on the doctor. His free hand came out of his jacket pocket, a kitchen knife firmly in his grip, as he mumbled quietly to himself.

'Oh Christ, no,' Smith blurted out as he backed down the stairs.

He didn't get far. Tony leapt forward, plunging the knife deep into the doctor's stomach. He pulled it out and punched the knife back in, repeating the process over and over. Dr Smith staggered back, shock and the brain's own defence system stopping him from feeling any pain. He fell to his knees, winded, unable to draw breath into his punctured lungs.

Blazer, you fucking bastard. I hope you rot in hell.

A smile spread across Tony's face as he muttered, 'End of level nineteen.'

The phone he still held to his ear clicked off, and Tony's pupils shrank back, exposing his light blue irises. The passive, blank look on his face changed to horrified as the sight of the doctor's bloody body in front of him registered on his conscious mind.

'Mr Smith, oh god, Mr Smith, can you hear me?' he said, crouching by the body. He reached forward to touch him, jumping at the sight of the bloody knife in his hand. 'Help me, somebody, please help me,' he shouted, throwing the knife to one side.

'What's happened?' said a neighbour running down from the fourth floor.

'I, I don't know. I was playing a game on my computer, then I was here and I found Mr Smith. I think I'm in shock. I don't remember how I got here. He's been stabbed. I, I must have picked up the knife. It's over there. I don't know, I don't remember.'

'Just sit on the stairs while I call the police and ambulance,' the neighbour said, his fingers on Dr Smith's neck, failing to get a pulse. He eyed Tony's bloodied hands suspiciously as he put the phone to his ear.

CHAPTER 5

Finishing work for the day, Nicki Miller climbed into her beaten-up Ford Ranger pickup truck. It was supposed to be magma red, but time and the elements left it a rusted and faded pink. She swore when it took four turns of the key to start, a cloud of diesel smoke rising from the rear of the truck.

'Great, yet another crap decision from my stupid ex-husband that I've ended up paying for,' she muttered, jamming the pickup into gear and heading off towards the supermarket.

Wandering around the aisles, Nicki picked up beers and pizzas and snacks for her brother and Danny for later on. She had plenty of time. Their flight wasn't due to land until 9:30 that evening, but she thought she'd check the live arrivals on her phone anyway, just in case there were any delays. She swore again when her phone wasn't in her bag, attracting a stern look from the old lady in the checkout queue. Embarrassed, Nicki pulled the plastic disc numbered 23 from her jeans pocket and realised she'd left it in the security locker at work. Normally she would have just left it until tomorrow, but the mobile was the only number Scott had to contact her when he landed.

Aw shit, I'll have to go back and get it.

She paid for the groceries and left. Hopping back into the pickup, she swore again when it chugged sluggishly into life on the third turn of the key. Leaving the car park, she turned back the way she came, heading back to work.

The sun fell below Blazer Games, leaving the building shrouded in an orange glow as she entered the car park. It was empty apart from a plain white panel van backed up to the loading doors at the rear and a couple of Toyota Land Cruisers parked near the entrance.

Nicki had never been back to work at night, but knew the place had 24-hour security. Parking right outside the entrance, Nicki walked up and peered through the glass. The reception desk was empty, and she couldn't see anyone moving around in the foyer. She tapped her pass card on the pad next to the door, and the doors slid open.

'Hello?' she said, sticking her head inside.

When no one answered, she moved inside and headed up the stairs towards the R&D department. The first-floor corridor was also empty, so she headed for the entrance door, placed her hand on the palm reader while the green light scanned her palm, and the door clicked open.

'Hello? Bill?' she said, entering the security room.

With nobody in sight and the empty building starting to give her the creeps, Nicki moved behind the desk and swung the door to the metal key box on the wall open. She took number 23 off the little hook and unlocked the locker with her phone in. With the plastic disc in her hand, Nicki looked around the desk. She picked up a pen and a post-it note and wrote: *Hi Bill, I just popped back to get my phone. See you tomorrow. Nicki Miller.*

After leaving the plastic disc on top of the note, Nicki

was just about to leave when she heard a noise from inside the R&D department. Thinking it might be the security guard, Nicki placed her hand on the palm reader and slid through the fire doors into the R&D room. There were only a few lights and the odd monitor on screensaver to light the room as she moved towards her desk. She was about to call out again when the door in the far corner that led to the offices and games suites burst open. An athletic-looking guy with shoulder length black hair, dressed in a blue boiler suit, backed into the room, pulling a packing crate on a pallet jack while a second man pushed from the other side.

'Bloody drone program. So we're fucking cleaners now,' said the man, pushing, his face illuminating as he moved under one of the ceiling lights.

Something about his tone and the look of him made Nicki duck down behind her desk. She told herself she was being stupid, hiding like a little girl, but his eyes were cold and lifeless in his hard as rock face. He sounded South African and had a tattoo covering his neck, ending just below the jawline. Peeping over the desk, Nicki saw the man with his back to her turn. He had a long face with alert eyes, like a hunter.

'Stop your whining and get the lift,' he said, waiting for the tattooed man to press the freight elevator button.

When the doors shut and the lift descended to the loading bay, Nicki took that as her cue to leave. She took a few steps towards the exit and stopped, a burning curiosity taking hold of her. She took another step towards the exit, then shook her head and turned, heading into the offices.

This is not a good idea, Nicki.

The offices were predictably office-like, which only made her question what she was doing even more. She poked her head into the observation room and its one-way window. The door was open to the games suite. After a quick check behind her to see if anyone was coming, Nicki went inside. There were two gaming chairs facing a gaming PC setup. The floor by the setup to the left was wet with a cleaner's bucket on wheels and mop to one side, its water and soap suds tinged red. A shattered monitor lay on the floor beside the gaming chair. Nicki squatted down to take a closer look. It was so beaten up that the screen was nearly bent in two.

What is that?

She touched the shattered surface, her finger recoiling at the realisation it was a large piece of skin and hair hanging off the bloodied shards of the screen's surface.

Oh god, shit, shit. I shouldn't be here.

Shaking, Nicki backed up and hurriedly scooted back through the offices into the R&D room. She did a quick check to make sure the two guys in boiler suits weren't around, and hurried out into the first-floor corridor, trying to rationalise what she'd seen as she went.

Someone must have had an accident and those guys are the night cleaners. That'll be it, just an accident. But what was the drone program?

'Excuse me, miss,' came a voice from behind her.

'Yes,' shrieked Nicki, jumping out of her skin as she turned.

Two serious looking men in dark suits that strained over their muscular physiques stood staring at her. One, a picture postcard Australian, blonde hair, blue eyes and a tan; the other an Aboriginal man with wavy brown hair and dark eyes.

'Can you tell us what you're doing here, miss?' said the blonde-haired guy.

'Er, sorry. Who are you?' said Nicki, hiding her nerves as she challenged them.

'Maaka Carter, I'm Mr Blazer's head of security,' he said, holding an ID card in front of her face.

'Oh, I see. I'm Nicki Miller. I work in the R&D department.'

'And what are you doing here at this time of night, Miss Miller?' said Maaka, fixing her with an intense stare.

'I was, er, just fetching my phone. I, er, forgot it and I'm expecting a call from my brother. He's flying in from Eng—'

'Good night, Miss Miller,' Maaka said firmly, cutting Nicki off mid-sentence.

'Right, er, good night,' she replied, taking the hint to walk hurriedly towards the stairs.

'Miss Miller,' came Maaka's shout from behind.

'Yes,' she said, turning impatiently.

'You have blood on your finger,' Maaka said, his voice showing a hint of menace.

'Yes, it's nothing. I cut it on the edge of the locker when I got my phone,' Nicki said, lying as she looked at the blood on her fingertip from the screen in the games room.

'Ok, you have a good night,' said Maaka, still staring at her.

Nicki turned without answering and hurried down the stairs and out the exit. She jumped in the pickup and turned the key.

'Come on, not now, you piece of shit,' she said through gritted teeth, giving a sigh of relief when it started fourth click.

'We need to see the boss,' said Maaka to his colleague as they watched Nicki drive off in a puff of diesel smoke.

CHAPTER 6

Driving out into the suburbs, Nicki's mind turned over and over what had just happened. She parked outside her house in Croydon, grabbed the groceries and carried them into the kitchen. By the time she'd put them away, the rational side of her brain had quietened the side that leaped to sinister goings on.

She opened her laptop and looked up the arrivals one last time. Flight BA0214 was on time. With an hour to kill, she checked her emails and clicked around Facebook looking at the latest funny animal videos until curiosity made her type in Danny Pearson. Plenty of results, but none for the Danny Pearson due to arrive with her brother shortly. She was about to close the laptop lid when curiosity made her type in Theodore Blazer drone program. No results linking the two together. Loads on Theodore Blazer billionaire, Blazer Games and Blink Defence Systems, and loads on toy drones, military drones, and where to buy a drone. She tried a few combinations, Blazer Games drone program, Blink Defence drone program, all of which brought the same underwhelming result. Checking her watch and losing interest, she closed the laptop lid and got ready to leave for the airport.

Comparing Blazer Games to Blink Defence Systems was like comparing an open prison to a maximum security prison. It was tucked behind a twelve-foot wall, a 24/7 manned security hut at the gate. The windows on the main building were all one-way privacy glass, and high-tech CCTV cameras adorned the top corners. Located toward the rear of the building was a secure command room. Only a handful of the employees had clearance or had ever seen inside. Theodore Blazer and Kyle Drago were checking the wall of screens in front of them. All links between them and Dr Smith were being erased. CCTV, phone history and bank transfers between the doctor and Blink Defence Systems erased from existence. They turned at the sound of Maaka and his men entering the room.

'Maaka, I didn't expect to see you back here tonight. For Christ's sake, relax, guys. You look like you're going to a hitman convention,' Theo said, pushing his shoulder length wavy hair out of his eyes.

'We ran into someone during the cleanup,' Maaka said, serious as ever, his stance military to attention.

'Go on,' Theo said, the smile dropping from his face.

'An employee, Miss Nicki Miller. She said she'd forgotten her mobile and had come back to retrieve it.'

'Nicki Miller?'

'Purple hair, about five foot six, programmer,' Kyle said, leaning in to talk quietly in Theo's ear.

'Ah yes. Well, did she see anything?'

'I can't be 100 percent sure, sir,' said Maaka, his voice still rock steady and unemotional.

'How exciting,' Theo said with childlike enthusiasm. 'Phil, CCTV feeds. Blazer Games from— Maaka, time?' he yelled, spinning on his heels.

'1920 hours.'

'Seven this evening, on the main screen please.'

'Yes boss.'

The centre screen burst into life with a cross grid of Blazer Games CCTV feeds. The time stamp in the corner of the feed sped along as Phil fast-forwarded the recordings until Nicki's pickup truck entered the car park at 19:06, at which point Phil slowed the feed to real-time playback, flicking the grid of feeds to the screen on the left, leaving the feed displaying Nicki filling the main screen.

'What on earth is she driving?'

'It's a Ford Ranger, sir,' said Phil.

'That was a rhetorical question, Phil,' said Theo, rolling his eyes.

The main screen kept changing as Phil changed the feeds to follow Nicki through the building until they watched her retrieving her phone from the security locker.

'There we go, all very innocent. She's just retrieving her phone,' said Theo, losing interest and turning away from the screen.

'Wait a minute,' said Kyle, tapping Theo on the shoulder.

'What?' said Theo, turning back to see Nicki sliding into the R&D department.

He watched her duck behind her desk as two of Maaka's men took the crate with the bodies in down in the lift to the loading bay. A frown creased Theo's forehead when Nicki went to leave, then turned back and went into the offices and games suite.

'Curiosity killed the cat, my dear. Now, what did you see in there?'

'I don't know, sir, we disabled the cameras in there to give you privacy for the test,' came Phil's voice over Theo's thoughts.

'It's another rhetorical question, Phil. Give me strength. Maaka, the place was cleaned up, right? Nothing for her to see?' said Theo with growing irritation.

'She had blood on her finger,' said Maaka in a blunt statement of fact.

Theo stood and stared at Maaka and his men for a long time. They stood motionless, staring back, neither intimidated by Theo nor defiant, just powerful, self-assured and lethal in their craft. He finally turned towards the front, looking at a freeze framed image of Nicki.

'Run her through Hercules. The meeting with the Americans is coming up. Make sure she's not working for anyone. I want to know everything about her, everything down to the colour of her underwear,' said Theo, walking towards the exit with Kyle. He stopped after a few paces. 'You do know that last bit was a joke, right, Phil?'

'Yes, boss.'

Theo continued a couple of paces, then stopped again. 'I've got twenty on white. Any takers? Brian, Jeff?'

'I'll take black,' Brian said, waving his hand in the air without taking eyes off his monitor.

'Go on then, I say blue,' said Jeff.

Smiling, Theo continued towards the exit. 'Keep an eye on her,' he said to Maaka as he passed.

'Yes sir,' replied Maaka, falling in behind Theo with his men and following him out.

CHAPTER 7

'm glad that's over. Even in a premier cabin, twenty hours in a flying corned beef tin is pushing it,' said Danny, running his hand through his unruly dark mop of hair while yawning.

'Absolutely. That's the longest time we've been in a confined space together without you trying to kill somebody,' said Scott with a chuckle.

'Don't worry, they haven't opened the doors yet. There's still time,' Danny said, giving Scott a murderous look before flashing him a grin.

'Oh look, I'm saved. I'll text Nicki to say we're here,' Scott said, nodding towards the flight attendant opening the heavy aeroplane door.

Scott's phone buzzed its reply as they made their way through passport control and headed for baggage reclaim.

'She's waiting in the arrivals hall for us,' he said, jostling for pole position as the luggage belt came to life, and suitcases starting appearing one by one through the plastic curtain, trundling their way towards them.

'Great. Ah, there's mine,' said Danny, spotting his old army kit bag.

'Can't you use a suitcase like a normal person?' said Scott, looking around for his two-thousand-pound Moncler Genius armoured suitcase.

'Don't worry, mate, if they've lost all your Armani, you can borrow a pair of my sweatpants,' Danny chuckled.

'Perish the thought, dear boy. Anyway, salvation is in sight,' said Scott, stooping down to grab his suitcase off the carousel.

Walking ahead of Scott, Danny moved through the nothing-to-declare customs area and on through the double doors to the arrivals hall. He scanned the faces of people waiting for the flight's arrival, trying to match the image in his head of a teenage Nicki to the surrounding faces.

'Well, well, well, Daniel Pearson, you've improved with age,' said a purple-haired woman to the side of him.

'Nicki! Christ, I didn't recognise you,' said Danny, looking her up and down.

'Yeah well, I'm not that skinny, flat-chested seventeen year old anymore. Where's Bill Gates?'

'Ha ha, hilarious. How are you, sis?' said Scott, catching up to them.

'All the better for seeing my big brother. Come here and give us a hug,' she said, pouncing on him.

They made their way out of the terminal and followed Nicki into the short stay car park. Scott's face turned into a grimace when she stopped beside the tatty Ford Ranger.

'Is it safe?'

'Yeah, well, safe-ish. Just throw your luggage in the back and get in the car,' said Nicki, getting in the driver's seat.

'What are you waiting for, Scott, the concierge to get

your bags?' said Danny, dumping his bag and getting into the front passenger seat.

'Well, aren't we the comedians tonight?' Scott muttered to himself, putting the suitcase in the rear of the pickup before getting in the back. 'Oh god, it's worse on the inside.'

'Yeah, well, you came out of your divorce with a bucketful of cash left over. I came out of mine with this shit car and a whole load of credit card debts. Come on, you bastard, start,' she said, turning the key for the third time before the engine fired up.

'Sorry, Nicki, I didn't know things were that tough. You should have told me, I could have helped you out,' said Scott, feeling bad for grumbling about the car.

'It's ok, it was my mess to sort out, but thanks for the offer. Anyway, I've got a good job now and I've paid off most of the debts that useless tosser left me,' she said, smiling at her brother as she looked behind and reversed out of the parking space.

It took about twenty minutes for them to drive into Sydney's Croydon suburb.

'Looks like a nice place to live,' said Danny, eyeing up the tidy streets and palm tree lined shopping parades.

'Yeah it is, the people are real friendly as well,' Nicki replied, turning into her street.

The hairs on the back of Danny's neck tingled. A Toyota Land Cruiser with blacked-out windows sat across the street as they pulled onto Nicki's drive. As they grabbed their bags and headed inside, he had the feeling he was being watched from behind the black glass. Following behind the others, Danny turned at the door and stared straight at the big car for a few seconds before glancing up and down the street. All the houses had drives with smaller family cars and plenty of space for a second car, so why was the expensive all-terrain vehicle parked on the road? Even if it was a visitor, surely they would park on the drive.

Stop being paranoid, you're just jet lagged, overtired and overthinking things.

Shaking it off, he closed the door and joined the others inside.

'Nice place, Nicki. I like the wallpaper. It matches the purple hair,' Danny said, grinning as he looked at the feature wall in the living room in a dark purple pattern.

'Why thank you,' Nicki said, flicking her hair with her hands and smiling back. 'You guys want a tinnie? I've got pizzas and snacks in.'

Scott and Danny both looked at Nicki with blank faces.

'Come on, guys, you know what a tinnie is.'

'Yeah, we know what a tinnie is. We're just messing with you.'

'A beer would go down very nicely, thank you, sis,' said Scott, returning to his phone to answer twenty hours' worth of missed calls and emails from the flight.

'Come on, bro, put the phone down, work can wait,' said Nicki, handing a cold beer to Danny and sliding another across the kitchen table to Scott.

'Sorry, last one, then I'll turn it off for the night. Never a normal day in the world of Miller Software Systems,' Scott said, moving his thumbs over the phone screen at lightning speed before hitting send.

'Yeah, well, I've had a pretty bloody weird day at work myself,' said Nicki, cracking open a beer for herself.

'Yeah, how's that?' said Danny, glancing behind him at the sound of a car engine, to see the Land Cruiser drive off through the living room window.

'Yes, do tell,' said Scott, putting his phone in his pocket.

In between cooking the pizzas, Nicki told them what happened when she'd returned to work to get her phone.

They listened, pausing the story for a couple of minutes to cut up the pizza and grab more beers. Scott shot Danny a look when Nicki described the men, the mention of a drone program and the shattered monitor covered in blood and bits of skin.

'Mmm, that is pretty strange. I'm sure there must be an innocent explanation for it,' said Scott, looking across at Danny's creased forehead and darkening eyes.

'Yeah, weird,' Danny finally said, not wanting to put Nicki on edge.

'Ah, forget it, I've got the week off so let's talk about what we're going to do while you're here,' Nicki said, raising her can to them. 'Cheers.'

'Cheers,' Danny and Scott said in return.

They drank, chatted and ate until jet lag and tiredness got the better of them. When Nicki had retired for the night, Scott put his head around the guest room Danny was in.

'What do you reckon about all that business at Nicki's work?'

'Nothing, Scott. Come on, you know what you're like, the first sign of anything odd and you think there's some big conspiracy afoot,' said Danny, yawning.

'Mmm, perhaps so, but I saw you looking at that big car with the blacked-out windows when we arrived, and I noticed the look on your face when Nicki talked about what had happened,' Scott said, not letting it drop.

'Good night, Scott,' Danny said, ignoring him.

'Ok, ok good night, Daniel,' said Scott, retiring to his own room.

CHAPTER 8

Looking across Sydney's famous Bondi Beach from the terrace of his $20 million penthouse apartment in North Bondi, Theodore Blazer clinked his champagne glass against an attractive blonde woman's glass.

'Cheers,' he said, never taking his eyes away from hers.

'Cheers,' she said, breaking eye contact to look out across the bay. 'So why are the Americans coming to see you on Monday?' she continued, her voice warm and inviting.

'Oh, aren't we well informed. But you know I can't tell you about that, Natasha. I pride myself on client confidentiality,' said Theo with a pause and a smile before continuing. 'So what comes next? Are you going to torture the truth out of me?'

'Come now, Theo, these are modern times. The Russians do not torture the truth out of people anymore. The Kremlin just wants to know why the US military recently paid $30 million to your shell company account in the Cayman Islands and what they are expecting you to do

COMMAND TO KILL

in return,' Natasha said, her arm extending along the back of the patio seating so she could caress the back of Theo's neck with her long manicured nails.

'What an absolute shame. I was quite looking forward to the torture. Anyway, I don't know why they're interested. The Kremlin knows full well Blazer Defence supplies state-of-the-art systems to the US government and has done so for many years. As for the Cayman Islands account, the US government—as does the Russian government—likes a certain amount of anonymity over classified purchases. Excuse me just one moment,' said Theo, getting up when his mobile rang and walking into the kitchen out of Natasha's earshot.

'Maaka.'

'There's been a development.'

'Elaborate,' said Theo, looking back over his shoulder at Natasha still sitting on the terrace.

'Miss Miller picked up two men from a British Airways flight from London tonight,' said Maaka, his tone flat, never changing.

'Interesting. Have we got eyes and ears?'

'No, they returned before we could bug the house.'

'Mmm shame, you think she's British Intelligence?' said Theo, putting a finger up to indicate one minute to Natasha.

'It's possible, sir. One of the men she picked up was definitely trained. He spotted the surveillance vehicle the second he arrived and scoped the area out like a pro.'

'Did you get a picture?' said Theo, ducking into his office and placing his hand on the palm reader beside the six screens mounted in an arc two high around the desk.

'Yes sir, Brian's running the photo through Hercules and pulling the flight passenger list now.'

'Good. Where are they now?' said Theo as the screens

33

burst into life with the words Theodore Blazer as he logged into Hercules.

'They've bedded down for the night at Miss Miller's.'

'Ok, keep an eye on them, I'll be in in the morning,' Theo said, bringing up the photos being analysed by Hercules. A grid of nine squares ran through faces to one side as the computer searched for a match.

'Yes sir,' said Maaka.

'Oh, and Maaka?' Theo said, before Maaka hung up.

'Yes sir.'

'Be discreet, the Americans visit on Monday seems to be attracting a lot of unwanted attention. I've got Natasha Shayk from the Russian Consulate sniffing about as well.'

'Yes sir, do you have any orders regarding Miss Shayk?'

'No, not at the moment. Goodnight Maaka,' Theo said, taking a last look at the pictures before logging out of Hercules.

'Problem?' said Natasha, smiling as Theo returned to the terrace.

'No, no. Now let me top your glass up and you can tell me all about the perverted and degrading things you're prepared to do to make me talk,' said Theo, picking the champagne bottle up and topping up her glass before sitting down next to her.

'I'm not a Cold War spy sent to seduce the secrets out of you,' said Natasha, laughing.

'What an absolute shame,' said Theo, placing his hand gently round the back of her neck as he came in to kiss her.

He stopped close to her lips, their blue eyes locking before she moved the small distance forward to kiss him. When they parted, Theo smiled. He took her hand, stood and led her inside towards the bedroom.

UNTITLED

9

The sound of music playing from somewhere beyond his room propelled Danny from a deep sleep to wide awake in a split second. Blinking the sleep away, he focused on his surroundings. His brain had to spin a few cogs before memory kicked in and reminded him where he was. Throwing his jeans and a t-shirt on, he padded down the hall to the open plan kitchen-cum-dining and lounge area. Nicki mopped the tiled floor with her back to him, her purple ponytail swishing from side to side as she sang along to the radio. Memories of her as a teenager dancing around the living room of her and Scott's parents' house made Danny smile. She was always full of energy and fun to be around; he was glad to see she hadn't changed too much over the years. It suddenly dawned on him that Nicki had turned into an attractive woman and he was staring. Shaking it off, Danny turned away and clicked the kettle on.

'Oh, you're up,' said Nicki, jumping as she turned to see him standing in the kitchen.

'Sorry, didn't mean to make you jump,' Danny said, picking a mug off the shelf and shaking it towards her in an offering.

'Yeah, I'll have a coffee. Here, I'll make it,' she said, smiling as Danny looked blankly around her kitchen for the coffee and sugar.

'Morning all, coffee for me please,' came Scott's cheery voice from the hallway.

Danny wandered around the living room as Nicki made the coffee, old habits were impossible to resist and with a flick of his eyes, Danny checked out the road for the Toyota Land Cruiser or any vehicles out of place. When none presented themselves, he stepped away and joined Nicki and Scott at the table.

'So what's the plan while you're here?' said Nicki.

'Well, my meeting with the MacIntyre Group isn't until Tuesday, so how about we do some sightseeing? I might even buy my little sister some lunch. Daniel, what about you?' Scott said with a smile.

'Er, I have to meet the two guys who are going to run the Sydney branch of Greenwood Security. It should only take a couple of hours. I could meet you for lunch,' said Danny, checking the time on his old G-Shock watch.

'Whereabouts is it?' said Nicki.

'It's a little office on George Street. Paul said it was just across from the train station.'

'That's close to the centre. I could drop you off and you could meet us for lunch later. There's a great bistro in the Queen Victoria building. It's a fifteen-minute walk along George Street from your office.'

'Sounds good, thanks, Nicki.'

A short time later, Nicki turned the key and swore once more at the pickup truck's inability to start first time. She crunched it into gear when it eventually fired up and drove Danny and Scott towards the city centre.

CHAPTER 9

After a palm scan to get through the first locked door and another one to unlock the second door, Theo strolled into Blink Defence Systems' command room.

'Morning, gentlemen. The sun outside this windowless box is shining, it's Saturday and I'm sure we would all like to be somewhere else. So tell me what have we got on Miss Miller and her friends, so we can all get back to our weekend?' said Theo in his usual upbeat manner.

'Nothing unusual on Nicki Miller. She came from England six years ago, got a job in a bar where she met, married and divorced some deadbeat Australian drummer. He drank too much, spent too much, then left her a load of debt,' said Phil, pinging Nicki's personal details up onto the main screen.

'How disappointing, and I got up early today for this. What about her two visitors? I take it Hercules found a match?' Theo said, brushing his wavy blonde hair out of his eyes.

The screen changed as Phil punched up night vision images of Danny and Scott as they got out of Nicki's pickup.

'Yes, this is where it gets interesting. The short one is her brother, Scott Miller, and yes, I do mean the Scott Miller of Miller Software Systems,' said Phil, barely hiding the excitement in his voice.

'Scott Miller! Saved London and the US from a terrorist cyber attack and financial ruin Scott Miller? How the hell did we miss that?' said Theo, frowning.

'Yep, that Scott Miller. When we hired Nicki Miller, she was still using her married name, Nicki Stapleton, so there was no obvious link. She reverted back to her maiden name just before her promotion to the R&D department.'

'Ok, ok, I'll let that one go, but for future reference, maiden names and family cross checks, people. Right, what about Mr Serious?' Theo pointed to the blown-up picture of Danny taken last night as he stared intensely at the lens hidden behind the blacked-out windows of the Toyota Land Cruiser.

'Daniel Pearson, official job, Director of Operations for London-based firm Greenwood Security. They have a branch opening here in Sydney.'

'How convenient. Anything else?' said Theo, still staring at the big screen.

'Eh, nothing you're going to like, boss. I'm putting it up now,' said Phil, his fingers dancing across the keyboard.

Theo watched as file after file opened across the screens, military records stacked up with either *Classified* or *Top Secret* against them. When they found an odd file they could open, its contents was so heavily redacted it made no sense, with only words like, and, the, and he, visible between the blacked out writing.

'What about after the military?'

'Coming up now.'

Phil closed and dragged the military files to a screen on one side before punching up another set of files.

'Jesus Christ, questioned by police over Russian Mafia murders, released after British Intelligence intervention. Arrested over terrorist explosion, case closed by MI6. Firearms offences, deaths, cases closed, MI6 again. The list goes on. Liaison to FBI, commendation for services to Great Britain. He was even awarded the Presidential Medal of Freedom by the former US President. Get me Maaka on the phone,' said Theo, his face serious as he clicked his fingers impatiently.

'Boss,' came Maaka's voice over the speakers a few seconds later.

'Are you still tracking the Miller woman?' said Theo.

'Yes boss,'

'Listen, I want you to be extra careful. We think they're working for British Intelligence. The big guy's name is Daniel Pearson. He's a pro, his file reads like a bloody superhero movie. Just keep an eye on them, ok? I've got the Russians taking an interest and now the British snooping around. I don't need anything to rock the boat before the General's visit on Monday,' said Theo, still looking tense.

'Yes boss. Pearson isn't with the other two. He met two men at the offices of Greenwood Security. Atama is tailing him. He could follow you across a desert and you'd never see him. The other two are at the Queen Victoria shopping centre. Karl is watching them,' said Maaka, his voice monotone and full of confidence as always.

'Good, good, carry on,' said Theo, signalling to Phil to cut the call. 'Right, who's on this weekend?'

'Brian and Jeff,' said Phil.

'Good. Brian, Jeff, call me if anything comes up. The rest of you, go and play computer games or read comics, or whatever you nerds do in your spare time,' said Theo, turning to leave.

CHAPTER 10

Thanks, guys, you seem to have everything under control. We can't do much more until the carpet fitters do their thing and the phones and broadband are up. When did you say they were coming, Leo?' said Danny in the empty office.

'Carpet's coming Monday, broadband and phones are on Tuesday,' said Leo, Greenwood Security's latest employee.

'Great, I'll come back Tuesday after the carpet's laid and help you put all the office furniture and PCs together. As long as the broadband goes in with no problem, I'll get Scott to come in Wednesday and sort the PCs out so they link with the London office. Thanks again, Leo, Ethan. It's been good to finally meet you both,' Danny said, shaking their hands before leaving them to lock up.

He wandered down George Street, enjoying the sun and warm air, the buildings changing as he walked from the four- or five-storey blocks to new skyscrapers fighting for position and height the closer to the centre of the city he got. An ice cold chill ran down his spine, and the hairs on the back of his neck stood up as the uneasy feeling he was being watched crept over him. Without slowing the pace or moving his head, Danny flicked his eyes from reflections in windows and doors to a van's back window as it drove past. There were people, yes. Anyone who set his senses tingling, no. Unable to shake the feeling, he ducked into a Starbucks and ordered a latte, watching the street through the shop window while the barista prepared his drink. Most people trained in the art of tailing someone would walk casually past the shop and wait down a side street or in a store further on. When the target continued their journey, the tail would move out and resume their tail. Apart from an elderly couple and a businessman in a suit with his phone glued to his ear, nothing.

'Your coffee, sir!'

'What? Oh, thanks,' Danny said, taking the drink.

He exited the shop, looking up and down the street as he left. Seeing nothing out of the ordinary, he decided he was jet lagged and over sensitive because of Nicki's story, and the blacked-out Toyota Land Cruiser last night. Shaking it off, he headed towards the Queen Victoria centre to meet Scott and Nicki.

'Pearson is heading your way, five minutes,' said Atama, tucked in behind an office entrance, peeping just far enough to watch Danny walk away from the coffee shop with one eye.

'Ok, I've got eyes on the other two. They're getting a table at a bistro on the second floor.'

'Be careful, he's good, very good. He nearly caught me

a couple of times. Keep well out of sight,' said Atama, moving out to follow Danny.

'Don't tell me how to do my job, Atama. He's good, he's good! I'm fucking good, ok,' came Karl's gruff response.

'Ok, ok, I'm just saying he knew he was being followed without even seeing me. He's sharp, alright,' said Atama, hanging up.

Danny spotted the Queen Victoria Building with little trouble. Its grandeur and historical style standing out in front of the backdrop of skyscrapers, it had similar features to London's St Pancras and Victoria train stations of the same period. He entered and wandered along the ornate tiled floor towards the escalator and a map of the centre. Finding the bistro on level 2, Danny rode up the escalator, checking discreetly below him as he continued, still trying to shake the feeling of being followed. He stepped off onto level 2 and headed for the bistro at the far end of the level. As he got closer, he could see Scott and Nicki waving to him from a table inside. He smiled back, catching an image in his peripheral vision as he did so; a big guy browsing in a gift shop to his left, wearing a light jacket with the collar turned up, his tattooed neck still visible over the collar. Continuing as if he hadn't seen him, Danny entered the bistro and joined Scott and Nicki.

'Everything go alright, Daniel?' said Scott, giving a wave to the waitress.

'Yes, everything went fine,' said Danny, his forehead creasing as he looked out of the window at the craft shop.

'Well, you could tell your face that, old man. What's so interesting out there?' said Scott, looking around outside.

At that moment Karl came out of the gift shop with a wrapped present in his hand. He turned quickly, careful to keep his back to the bistro as he headed away.

'Nicki, see that big guy, light jacket, collar turned up, is that the same guy you saw yesterday at work?'

Nicki turned and looked at the back of Karl as he continued to walk away.

'God, yeah, I think it is, if I could just see his face,' she said, gasping when a glimpse of Karl's tattooed neck showed over his collar. 'Yeah, that's him, definitely.'

'Well, what do we do?' said Scott, swinging his head from the window to Danny and back again.

'Nothing, it's just a weird coincidence. Let's order lunch, I'm starving,' said Danny, dismissing it.

'Hmm, you always tell me you don't believe in coincidences,' said Scott, watching the figure of Karl disappear down the escalator.

'Maybe so, but what else am I going to do? Chase down some bloke who may, or may not be one of the cleaners Nicki saw the other night, or may, or may not be one of the men in the Toyota Land Cruiser outside Nicki's. The cleaners who were doing what in the office? Oh yes, cleaning,' said Danny, a little more forcefully than he intended.

'OK, let's forget it and order,' said Scott, smiling as the waitress approached.

'Hang on a minute. What Toyota Land Cruiser outside my house?' said Nicki, looking straight at Danny.

'It's probably nothing. There was a car on the street when we got back yesterday. It looked a little out of place and drove off when we went inside. Right, let's order,' said

Danny as casually as he could before lifting the menu to distract Nicki from the conversation.

Nicki sat, not knowing what to say, her brain ticking over too many questions that she didn't have answers for.

'Don't worry, sis, you're a Miller. As Daniel is always reminding me, we have a habit of getting carried away with things. Now let's all relax and enjoy lunch.'

'He made you,' said Atama, appearing out of nowhere as Karl stepped off the escalator onto the ground floor.

'No, he didn't, and don't fucking sneak up on me like that. I'm liable to put a bullet in that little pea brain of yours,' growled Karl, marching towards the exit.

'He fucking made you and you know it,' said Atama, smiling as he followed.

Karl stopped dead in front of Atama, his hand on the butt of his gun under his jacket as he leant his face in close to Atama's.

'Say he made me again, I fucking dare you,' Karl said in a low, gruff voice.

The two men stood with eyes locked on each other. A blade clicked open as Atama pressed the release on the flick knife in his hand, while Karl tightened his grip, ready to pull his gun. After a tense minute, both men backed away from each other. Karl released his grip on the gun and Atama folded the blade away.

'They're going nowhere up there, let's go and put eyes and ears into the woman's house,' said Karl, resuming his walk to the exit.

Atama followed after a few seconds.

'Come on, hurry up, you fucking Kiwi wanker,' said Karl over his shoulder.

'Fuck off, you South African arsehole,' Atama grumbled back.

CHAPTER 11

Lunch and the afternoon went by quickly. The three of them reminisced as Nicki took them sightseeing around the city. Scott and Nicki relaxed and pushed the strange events of the two days to the back of their minds; Danny, although relaxed and free from the sense of being followed, couldn't help checking his surroundings every time Scott and Nicki weren't looking, but nothing out of the ordinary presented itself. They got back to Nicki's as the sun dipped low in the sky, its rays beaming in through the living room window as they entered the kitchen.

'You guys want a beer?' Nicki said, heading for the kitchen fridge.

'I'll have one in a minute, sis. I'm just going to have a shower and freshen up a bit, if that's alright?' said Scott, heading for the guest room.

'Of course it is. Here, let me get you a towel,' said Nicki, following Scott up the hall.

Danny stood just inside the front door, his face hard as granite. He bobbed down on his haunches and meticulously scanned the kitchen floor. As the sun's last rays hit its surface, a number of faint boot prints dulled the shine on the tiles that Nicki had mopped that morning. Noting their direction, Danny stood and studied the kitchen.

Not a thing out of place, so why were you here?

'Did you want that beer?' Nicki said, coming back into the kitchen.

'Er, yeah, thanks,' Danny replied, turning a smile onto his face.

Taking the bottle off her, he moved casually to the corner of the kitchen and leant on the counter.

'Are you hungry? I've got some steaks I could throw on the barbie,' said Nicki, opening the fridge.

'Yeah, that'd be great,' Danny forced a smile as Nicki pulled the steaks out and headed for the barbecue in the back garden.

The second she was out of sight, he stretched up and ran his fingers along the top of the kitchen cabinets, stopping when he touched something small. He brought it down and turned it towards himself, looking down at a tiny camera lens. Frowning, he tossed it in the kitchen sink and turned the tap on, killing it dead.

Right, you wouldn't put one up without a backup, so where are you?

Looking around for obvious places to hide another camera, Danny spotted a slither of a tiny black box on top of the air conditioning unit mounted high on the living room wall. He dried off the camera from the sink and walked over. Standing underneath the air con unit, he stretched up on tiptoe and got his fingers on the box. When he brought it down, it was an identical unit. Danny killed it in the sink, then dried it off and put both units and a knife from the kitchen drawer in his pocket before joining Nicki on the garden patio.

'Those smell good,' he said.

'They most certainly do,' said Scott, coming out to join them.

'Thanks, guys. I've got salad and pasta in the fridge. Here, look after these and I'll get them,' Nicki said, handing the barbecue control over to Scott.

'I'm just going to change my top,' Danny said, excusing himself.

When he was in his room, he pulled the tiny remote cameras out and prised the lid off one of them with the kitchen knife.

Let's have a look at what we've got here: long-life lithium battery, camera lens, microphone and Wi-Fi unit. They must have hacked Nicki's router to stream the feed. Expensive kit. They obviously think she knows something, but what?

Looking at his watch, he worked out it was 9ish Saturday morning back in England. Turning the camera devices over in one hand with his phone in the other, Danny sat on the bed contemplating what he should do.

'Fuck it, they owe me a few favours,' he muttered to himself as he pressed dial.

'Daniel, I haven't heard from you in a while. What can I do for you?'

'I need a favour, Edward,' Danny said bluntly.

'I'm guessing it's not, can I feed the cat while you're away type of favour?' Edward replied.

'Would I be calling the Chief of the Secret Intelligence Service if it was?'

'No, I guess not. Go on,' Edward said, intrigued.

'I'm in Australia with Scott and his sister. We arrived yesterday and had surveillance on the house. A pro tailed me around the city today. I never got eyes on him, but I know he was there. When we got back to Nicki's, I found two surveillance devices, military grade, very high spec.'

'Do you think it's someone from your past after you?' said Edward, spinning a long list of candidates through his mind.

'No, it's something to do with Nicki's work at Blazer Games. It's owned by the Australian billionaire Theodore Blazer, he also owns Bl—'

'Blink Defence Systems, yes I know who he is. But why would he be interested in Scott's sister?' said Edward, struggling to understand the link.

'I don't know. She went back into work late last night to pick her phone up and witnessed what sounds like a clean-up crew. I have a feeling they think she knows something she shouldn't,' said Danny, pausing as Scott shouted from outside that the steaks were ready.

'Ok, but I'm not sure what we will have at MI6 on him.'

'Then call Howard. Remind him he owes me,' said Danny with a determination in his voice.

'I think you mean David Tremain.'

'Howard, David Tremain, or whatever the hell he's calling himself this week. Yes, the Minister of Defence, call him,' Danny said impatiently.

'Ok, ok, I'll call him and come back to you,' replied Edward before hanging up.

Danny tucked the devices in his bag, forced himself to look more relaxed, and went out to join the others.

'Whoa, what's he doing? Jeff, are you seeing this?' said Phil, throwing the camera feed from Nicki's house up onto the main screen in the command room.

'Has he dropped something?' said Jeff, looking at Danny squat down as he looked across the kitchen floor.

When Danny stood up, he looked around then stared straight into the lens, the intensity of his stare making Jeff and Phil flinch in their chairs. Tense seconds later Nicki left the room and the next thing they knew, Danny was staring down the lens before throwing the camera in the sink. It blinked and crackled before the feed went dead.

'Arr, shit,' Phil said, watching Danny grab the second device and kill that one as well. 'How the hell did he know they were there?'

'I don't know, but someone better let the boss know,' said Jeff, placing his headphones on quickly and turning away from Phil as he tapped away on his computer.

'What! Really, so that someone's me then? Thanks, Jeff,' muttered Phil as he pressed Theo's contact number.

'Saturday evening, guys, this better be good. I have a table booked at Automata,' came Theo's voice over the speakers.

'It's Pearson. Atama is sure he knew he was being followed and that he made Karl. They abandoned the surveillance,' said Phil.

'Ok, that's bad, but there was no interaction between them?'

'No, boss, but there's more. Maaka's men put two surveillance devices in the Miller woman's house. Pearson found them both in minutes,' said Phil looking across at Jeff who was waving at him.

'Hang on, we've got cell activity in the house.'

'Let's hear it then,' said Theo impatiently.

'Just a minute, boss, we're hacking the network now,' said Phil, watching Jeff as he tapped furiously on his keyboard.

'Hurry up, or we'll miss it,' demanded Theo.

'Coming through now,' said Jeff, patching the audio to the speakers.

'Then call Howard. Remind him he owes me,' came Danny's voice.

'I think you mean David Tremain,' replied Edward.

'Howard, David Tremain, or whatever the hell he's calling himself this week. Yes, the Minister of Defence, call him.'

'Ok, ok, I'll call him and come back to you,' came Edward's voice before the line went dead.

'I knew it, the bloody British. They called me crazy when I took the idea to them two years ago, but now the Americans are taking me seriously. They want my drone project,' said Theo angrily.

'What do you want us to do, boss?' said Phil.

'Nothing, we do nothing until the General signs the project off on Monday. Once they've gone, I'll show the British what the drone project can really do.'

CHAPTER 12

A couple of hours after Danny's call to Edward, his phone buzzed with an incoming text.

Thank you for your enquiry.
I can confirm the goods you have ordered will be delivered tomorrow morning.

The message had no ID, but he knew it was from the government man and his former handler who he'd only known as Howard for so many years. Howard had retired from his former covert role and was now the Minister of Defence under his real name, David Tremain.

With nothing more he could do for the time being, Danny relaxed a little with Scott and Nicki before turning in for the night. He woke early, his head in a different time zone and his mind still tumbling through unanswered questions. Pulling a creased pair of running shorts and an equally creased t-shirt out of his old army kit bag, he dressed, threw on his trainers and went for a run.

The early morning air was cool, and he was pleased to

see there weren't any unusual people or vehicles near Nicki's house. He ran through the neat suburban roads of Croydon with its predominantly single-storey houses, then around Wanga Park before heading back to Nicki's as the temperature started to rise. Hot and sweaty, Danny stripped out of his t-shirt as he walked up the path to Nicki's house. He entered to find Nicki standing in the kitchen in a revealing nightshirt. She stood awkwardly for a moment, the sight of knife, shrapnel and bullet wound scars on Danny's muscular torso catching her by surprise.

'Morning, er, I'm just going for a shower,' Danny finally said, looking away quickly when he realised he was staring at Nicki in her nightshirt as she stared back at him.

'Huh, oh, yeah,' she said, unable to stop herself from taking a peep at his back as he walked down the hall.

He returned twenty minutes later to find Nicki dressed and chatting to Scott out on the patio.

'Ah, here he comes. Britain's answer to the missing link. Morning, Daniel,' said Scott, raising a coffee cup to Danny.

'Said the seventies porn star lookalike. Morning, Scott,' said Danny with a grin.

'I'll have you know I would have made a great porn star,' said Scott, brushing his floppy hair back and returning the grin.

'God, you two haven't changed a bit since high school,' said Nicki, getting up at the sound of the doorbell.

'It's alright, I'm up, I'll get it,' Danny said, moving down the hall towards the front door.

Approaching with caution, Danny darted across to the kitchen and slid a carving knife out of the knife block, holding it blade up, concealing it from view with his forearm. With nobody in sight through the front window or glass in the door, Danny turned the latch and opened it. A parcel sat on the doormat. He looked around. No one in sight in the street, no vehicles driving in either direction. Picking it up, Danny closed the door and put the knife back on his way through to the back garden.

'What's that?' said Nicki.

'I don't know. It's from someone I used to work for,' said Danny, opening it up.

'Howard?' said Scott sitting upright, his interest piqued.

'Or David Tremain, take your pick,' said Danny, pulling out an encoded Inmarsat satellite phone similar to ones he'd used in the SAS.

It rang in his hand, making him jump.

'Hello,' Danny said, pressing the accept button.

'Mr Pearson, I presume,' came the type of arrogant, authoritative voice Danny knew only too well.

'And you are?'

'You may call me Simon. Think of me as the new Howard,' said Simon, pausing for his words to make maximum impact.

'Cut the niceties, Simon, what have you got for me?' said Danny, not hiding his disdain for secretive government agents.

'My, my, aren't we the touchy one. To business then. The events you have been encountering since Miss Miller's late night discovery at Blazer Games are of interest to our department, as is Mr Blazer himself. I can't reveal too many details, but Mr Blazer approached the UK defence committee some time ago with some decidedly out of the box ideas for a worldwide network of sleeper assets. Drone soldiers, I think he called it, deployable anywhere, at any time. The defence committee quite rightly directed Mr Blazer back from whence he came, but not without keeping tabs on his activities. We have no direct proof that Mr Blazer is up to anything, but our sources say the Kremlin

COMMAND TO KILL

has placed a known operative at the Russian Consulate in Sydney. Coincidently, the rather attractive operative has been seen out and about with Mr Blazer several times this week. Added to that, a US General from a department the US government doesn't think we know about, is flying out to meet Mr Blazer as we speak, all incredibly hush-hush. All we need is the Chinese to turn up and the party can really get started.'

'Well, this is all incredibly interesting. But what the fuck has this got to do with Nicki, Scott or myself,' said Danny, his patience wearing thin.

'Absolutely nothing. But consider this: Theodore Blazer developed the computer systems the FBI and the Pentagon use, and has the identical capability at the Blink Defence building, hence the encoded satellite phone. It's entirely possible he knows about your past links to the UK's intelligence services, and that association could well cast a suspicious shadow over Miss Miller's uninvited arrival to the office party or whatever was taking place there,' said Simon to silence as Danny turned the information over in his mind.

'Mmm, ok, so you don't think we're in any danger?' Danny finally said.

'The world is a dangerous place, Mr Pearson. We are all in a certain amount of danger, but I have no information to say Theodore Blazer is responsible for any misadventures.'

'Ok, thanks, what about the sat phone?' Danny said.

'Keep hold of it for now. If anything develops, press 1 to contact me. My predecessor gave you a glowing report. We could use a man like you,' said Simon, with a self-assured smugness.

'No, you couldn't,' growled Danny, hanging up without waiting for an answer.

'Well, that sounded a little intense. Do be a good fellow and tell us what the hell is going on,' said Scott.

'Short answer, the powers that be don't think we're in any danger. They think Blazer probably ran a check on us through Blink after his security detail saw us coming back from the airport. Our links to British intelligence, and Nicki being at the office when she shouldn't have been there, probably prompted Blazer to have his security team check us out,' said Danny to the two blank faces staring at him.

'Well, thank god for that. I think that calls for another beer,' said Scott, breaking into a smile.

'What should I do about work?' said Nicki, confused.

'There's nothing to do. You don't even know that anything untoward even happened. Enjoy your week's holiday and go back next week as normal,' said Danny, smiling to reassure her. 'Grab me one of those while you're out there, Scott.'

'Absolutely. Sis?' Scott shouted on his way to the fridge.

'Yeah, go on then,' she said, finally relaxing.

CHAPTER 13

'Morning, gentlemen, I need everybody on their A-game today. Phil, anything to report on our English friends over the weekend?' said Theo.

'After Pearson found the surveillance devices, I accessed the US satellite network. Nothing of interest Saturday night, but I got lucky Sunday morning,' said Phil, throwing images up on the main screens.

'Great images, where are these from?' said Theo, looking at time-lapsed images of a car pulling up a little way from Nicki's house, the passenger getting out and putting a box on the doorstep before getting back in the car and driving off.

'A Keyhole-class satellite. Phil tapped it as it passed over yesterday morning,' said Kyle.

'Way to go, Phil.'

Razor sharp images of Danny talking on the phone in Nicki's garden filled the screen, its distinct antenna giving it away as a satellite phone.

'A satellite phone, how very subversive. Right, get it off the screen. Our guests will be here soon, so no mention of the English. Let's concentrate on the demonstration. Where is our target?'

'She left the house for work five minutes ago. Maaka has Atama and Karl on them,' said Brian, from a desk behind Theo.

'Good, let's hope they don't fuck it up like they did Miss Miller and co.'

'Your guests are here,' said Jeff, pinging up an image of three black cars pulling up at the security gate.

'Thank you, Jeff. Showtime. With me, Kyle,' said Theo, brushing his shoulder length, wavy blonde hair back and heading out with Kyle to meet them.

Theo danced lightly down the stairs with Kyle in tow, just in time to see his two guests enter the foyer. Four black-suited personal security agents complete with shades and earpieces followed close behind.

'Gentlemen, welcome,' Theo said, walking past the security baggage scanner and through the metal detector. 'General Simmons, Agent Johnson, very good to see you again. This is my Operations Director, Kyle Drago,' Theo said before they all shook hands.

'Thank you, Mr Blazer, I hope you have something good to show us,' said the General, direct as ever.

'All will be revealed, if you'd like to follow me. Open the gate please, I imagine the General's, er, colleagues would light that up like a Christmas tree,' said Theo, pointing to the metal detector as the security man opened a gate to one side. 'Would your colleagues like to wait in the canteen while we continue business in the command room?'

The General turned and nodded to the steely faced men.

'Kyle, would you mind showing these gentlemen to the canteen?'

'Of course, follow me please,' said Kyle, leading the security detail off down the corridor.

The General and Agent Johnson followed Theo to the command room and waited while the panel on the wall scanned Theo's palm before the door lock clicked open. They entered a small foyer with an identical locked door ahead of them.

'If you please,' said Theo, pointing back at Agent Johnson, holding the door open behind him. 'The door won't open until we shut the outer door, stops anyone sliding in behind you,' said Theo, before placing his hand on a second palm scanner once Agent Johnson let the door click shut.

He led them into the command room and stopped in front of the array of giant screens.

'Ok, Blazer, I'm going to lay it on the line. Department 23 has invested a lot of money for this research, and so far we've had precious little results. You haven't given us any progress reports, hell, we've had nothing to say this project even exists. If I don't see anything today, I'm pulling your funding and going with one of your competitors,' said the General, his face hard and eyes boring into Theo who smiled back as Kyle entered the room and took his place next to him.

'No, General. You won't. There are a number of organisations who have tried and failed with mind control programs, including your own government, General. Like your government, they all discovered you cannot effectively coerce or drug large numbers of people into mind control, and you lack the delivery system. Blazer Games' blockbuster release, Command to Kill, has over eighty-five million players worldwide. These players use more of the prefrontal cortex part of the brain than in any other activity. In the heightened state of game play, we can exert neurological changes to their brains. We can plant subtle choices to select candidates. These choices lead the most susceptible players through a series of levels, each one re-enforcing our control over them until they are completely primed into what we call the drone state. Around sixteen percent of players will follow the gaming levels to the end. That's thirteen point five million players worldwide,' said Theo with a smile.

'But how's that undetectable? A program like that would be traced back to the game. It'd be a national scandal. You'd all go to jail,' said Agent Johnson, stunned by what Theo was saying.

'Cloud based, Mr Johnson. The advanced levels are real time streamed by our system, the player has no physical copy, no proof. The choices taken by susceptible players take them off the main game and to levels only they see. These levels are all securely hosted here on our internal servers.'

'Are you bullshitting me, Blazer? What kinda fool do you take me for? You've had millions of United States dollars and you spin me this crap,' said the General, his face reddening with anger.

'I assure you, General. My father built this company. When he died I took Blink Defence into the twenty-first century, supplying the most powerful intelligence organisations in the world. My father was no bullshitter and neither am I,' said Theo, his face serious and eyes locked defiantly with the General's. The room hung in uneasy silence for a long few seconds before Theo's face softened and his million-dollar smile returned. 'Now, how about a demonstration to lighten the mood?'

'Ok, but this better be good, Blazer,' growled the General.

COMMAND TO KILL

'Phil, status report on the target please,' said Theo, ignoring the General.

'Target is at the Terrace Restaurant on the edge of Domain Park, opposite the art gallery. I'm accessing the restaurant's CCTV now,' said Phil, tapping away furiously at his keyboard.

The main screen burst into life as multiple camera feeds slowly popped up in a cross grid of live video pictures of the restaurant.

'Ah, there she is. Bring up camera eight please, Phil,' said Theo.

Camera eight's feed filled the screen with the image of an attractive blonde woman sitting at a table outside. She looked up as the waiter approached to take her order.

'Alfresco dining, how delightful. Who have we got close?' continued Theo, a hint of excitement entering his voice.

'We've got four drones within a three-mile radius,' said Brian from the other side of the room.

'Mmm, find out what vehicles are registered to them.'

'I've got two with vehicles, a Nissan Cherry and a Ford Transit,' said Brian a minute later.

'We have control of Transit man's phone?'

'Yes boss.'

'Whoa, wait, what's going on here?' said Agent Johnson, stepping forward.

'I'm going to kill the target by getting our test drone to drive his van into her,' said Theo matter of fact.

'Kill, you can't just— Who is this woman?' stammered Agent Johnson in disbelief.

'A Russian FSB spy, Natasha Shayk, and I wouldn't feel too bad for her. She'd kill you in a heartbeat if you got in her way. Miss Shayk was responsible for administering the lethal dose of Polonium 210 to your defecting Russian

63

scientist Mr Klinck and his family last May,' said Theo, as all eyes fell on Agent Johnson, pausing the demonstration.

It was the General who broke the stalemate. 'Hold your tongue, Johnson, Department 23 was set up to secure the highest weapons tech the world has to offer. It's our job to ensure the safety of the United States of America, and that's exactly what we're doing here. Keep your opinions to yourself and remember who's in charge here. Now carry on with the demonstration, Mr Blazer,' he said, stepping in front of Johnson.

CHAPTER 14

"Morning, Joe, usual?"

'Morning, Brenda, yeah, usual and a blueberry muffin,' said Joe, looking through the glass counter in his favourite coffee shop.

His phone rang with no ID as Brenda turned her back to him and steamed the milk for his latte.

'Hello.'

'New orders from command.'

Joe stood rooted to the spot, his pupils went wide, almost covering the irises.

'I have a mission for you, Joe. I need you to get in your van now. Do you understand?'

'Yes,' Joe said in a low voice, before turning and walking out of the coffee shop, the phone still to his ear.

'Joe, your coffee, Joe,' Brenda called out after him.

'Look at your phone, Joe, you will see a picture of your target,' the voice said as Joe climbed into his van. Moving the phone away from his head, Joe saw the CCTV picture of Natasha Shayk sitting outside the restaurant. 'Do not put your seatbelt on Joe. Start the engine and follow the directions to the target. When you see her, you will accelerate and drive your van into her, do you understand Joe?' came the voice as the phone switched to loudspeaker and the screen changed to maps.

'I understand,' said Joe, putting the van into gear and pulling away.

'Visual,' said Theo impatiently.

'Coming up, boss, the van will be in sight in twenty seconds on the left screen,' said Phil as a series of traffic camera images burst into life.

All eyes focused on the College Street and Park Street junction, top left. Twenty seconds later the white Transit van crossed the junction and disappeared off to the right-hand side of the picture.

'Centre screen, thirty seconds to target,' continued Phil as the van came into view, turning down Art Gallery Road.

They watched the van disappear from view, to be picked up on the next screen by a CCTV camera on the Art Gallery building on the opposite side of the road to the restaurant. A smile crept onto Theo's face and his eyes sparkled as the van sped up, mounting the kerb and appearing on the restaurant's CCTV as it headed straight towards the circular shaped building and Natasha as she sat outside. She turned her head at the sound of the approaching van, horror written on her face as it crashed up the restaurant steps in an explosion of wood, bits of van and headlight glass. Natasha had no time to move out of its way, it struck her dead centre, carrying her backwards into the fixed seating that ran around below the restaurant windows.

Natasha's ribs snapped and her internal organs crushed, forcing blood out of her mouth and nose as the van flattened her, destroying the seating before hitting the restaurant wall. The deceleration from forty to zero in the blink of an eye sent Joe crashing through the windscreen. Already unconscious, he flew over Natasha's body. His neck snapped as his head hit and shattered the restaurants toughened glass window before bouncing off a dining table inside.

'Goodbye, Natasha,' Theo whispered coldly before the face he presented to the public returned. 'Excellent, mission accomplished. A random accident, no link between the driver and victim, and no reprisals from the Russians. Delete all the driver's phone activity and network provider records for the last twenty minutes please, Phil,' Theo said, turning to face Agent Johnson and the General, the CCTV pictures from inside the restaurant continuing to display the chaos and screaming diners behind him.

'Yes boss.'

'Gentlemen,' said Theo.

'This has gone far enough. Research is one thing, but if you think the US government will sanction the control and killing of innocent civilians, you are seriously deluded. You've got to close this down immediately,' said Agent Johnson, stepping forward angrily.

'Hush your mouth, Johnson, you're overstepping your authority,' said the General, shooting Johnson a challenging look that made him back down. 'Ok, Blazer, you've made your point. How soon can you make this operational?'

'It already is, General,' said Theo, shooting Johnson a smug smile.

'Good, I'll have our shell company deal with the payment to your account in the Cayman Islands as before.'

'Perfect. Once it is received, Kyle will set up a secure link between our command centre and yours and my team will be at your disposal,' said Theo, extending his hand.

'Oh and Blazer, due to the nature of this project, this ever gets leaked out, Department 23 never existed. You'll be on your own,' said the General, shaking Theo's hand.

'Of course, General,' Theo turned and extended his hand to Agent Johnson, who ignored the gesture, turning away to leave.

'Mr Drago will see you out,' said Theo, unperturbed.

Theo watched them go, waiting until the door clicked shut before he let out a cheer.

'Good work, guys. Phil, Brian, you were outstanding. Let's wrap it up and go get drunk. You've all earned your bonuses today,' said Theo, walking around shaking hands and patting backs.

'What about Miss Miller and her friends?' said Phil.

'Tomorrow, Phil, we'll deal with that tomorrow.'

CHAPTER 15

'My, my, you scrub up well,' said Nicki, looking up at her brother as he entered the kitchen in a light brown Prada suit.

'Oh thanks, it's just something I threw together,' chuckled Danny, looking up from his breakfast.

'Yes, Daniel, your t-shirt is stunning. It puts my suit to shame,' said Scott, moving to the living room window.

'Thanks, Scotty boy, I can lend you one for your meeting if you like.'

'Do you two ever stop?' said Nicki, sitting down opposite Danny with a bowl of muesli.

'Very rarely, my dear. Ah, there's my car. Right, I'm off to be wined and dined by the MacIntyre Group. I'll see you both this evening,' said Scott, waving to the driver of the MacIntyre Group's corporate limousine.

'Yeah, see you, mate,' said Danny, waving over his shoulder.

'Bye,' Nicki said, watching him go.

'Right, I'm off as well. I'm going to get the train into

the city. Are you going to be alright here?' Danny said, noticing the apprehension on Nicki's face.

'Er, yeah, I suppose. It's just been a weird few days. No, I'm fine,' she said, trying to convince herself.

'You can come with me if you like. I'm only building desks and setting up PCs. If you're lucky I might even pay for lunch. Up to you,' Danny said, knowing the answer from the look on her face.

'Only if you don't mind.'

'Nah, I'd be glad of the company.'

'Great, and don't worry about the train. I'll drive,' she said, getting up with renewed enthusiasm.

'I've changed my mind. You can stay here,' Danny said, smiling.

'Oi, my driving's not that bad.'

'Morning Kyle. Do you ever go home?' said Theo, entering the command room with the morning newspaper under his arm.

'No,' replied Kyle dryly.

'That's why I like you so much. Now what's going on with our English friends?'

'A car came to pick up Scott Miller this morning. We tried to access his laptop and phone but he's running some very sophisticated encryption software. Hercules is still on it. The car is registered to the MacIntyre Group out in Penrith, so we can only assume he's got some business with them,' said Kyle, clicking his fingers to Phil who put up a map with a tracking dot blinking for the location of the MacIntyre car.

'Ok, what about his sister and the hired muscle?'

'They left in Miss Miller's Ford Ranger around an hour ago. We tracked it to a Wilson multi-storey car park on Thomas Street. They're currently at the new Greenwood Security offices on George Street, we have a—' Kyle clicked his fingers at Phil again, 'CCTV feed from a bar opposite,' he continued as the image of the Greenwood Security office appeared on the centre screen in front of them.

'What are they doing? Can we zoom in?' said Theo, squinting at the image.

'Doing it now, boss.'

'No, it's still fuzzy. Can we enhance it?'

Phil's fingers danced over the keys, and the image got marginally clearer.

'That's the best I can do. The camera's pretty low resolution.'

'Ok, ok, what are they doing?' Theo said, focusing on the figures moving about inside the office.

'It looks like they are building desks,' said Kyle.

'Oh! How very DIY of them. Well, while our friends are preoccupied, get me a list of all operatives in the vicinity. Let's give the drone program a proper test, shall we?' said Theo with a childlike grin on his face.

'Do you think that's wise so soon after the agreement with the General?' Kyle said softly so the others in the room couldn't hear.

'General or no general, this is my project and I'll protect it however I see fit,' hissed Theo, his face shifting into a rare look of anger before shifting back into outward calmness.

'As you wish,' said Kyle, moving over to a PC console.

'Why have I got this piece left over?' said Nicki, sitting on the floor with a metal bar in one hand and the desk instructions in the other.

'I don't know. I'll have a look after I find out why I've got two of these left over,' said Danny, holding up two L-shaped brackets with a grin.

Hopping to his feet, Danny picked up the desk he'd been building and plonked it down on the new carpet over the floor socket, ethernet, and phone connection panel.

'You two be alright for a bit? I promised Nicki some lunch,' said Danny to Leo and Ethan.

'Yeah, we're fine,' said Leo, unpacking a brand new monitor for the desk.

'Great, I'll get coffee and cakes on the way back.'

'Sounds good to me,' shouted Ethan from the room out back.

'Ok, we'll see you in a bit,' Danny said, offering a hand to Nicki and pulling her up off the floor with ease.

Their eyes locked as she stood upright. Neither of them moved for a few awkward seconds until Danny realised he was still holding her hand.

'Er, right, lunch,' he said, releasing her hand and turning away, a little embarrassed.

'Good, I'm starving,' Nicki replied, chuckling at his embarrassment as she followed him out the door.

'I can hear you, you know,' Danny said without turning round.

'I'm only teasing,' she said, moving up and linking her arm through his as they walked along the pavement.

He was about to answer her when the hairs on the back of his neck stood up. His eyes flicked left and right, looking for the source of danger he felt. None presented itself. A scraping sound from above made him look up just in time to see a washing machine tipping over a balcony four floors above them before hurtling down in their direction. Danny dragged Nicki back just in time to see the washing machine whizz past his eyes, hitting the pavement in an explosion of glass, plastic, and twisting metal.

'What the hell?' Danny said, looking up to see a huge overweight guy looking directly at him from the balcony above.

There was something wrong with his expression. His eyes looked vacant, and his face was devoid of expression as he muttered something to himself. To Danny's surprise, he swung his legs over the balcony and, without taking his eyes off them, he jumped off with his arms and legs out like a skydiver.

Pushing Nicki behind him, Danny stepped back. The man's image seemed to hang in midair above him before it hit the pavement beside the washing machine with a sickening slapping sound. Completely dumbfounded, Danny crouched down and felt the guy's neck for a pulse. With blood oozing out of his ears, nose and mouth, Danny wasn't surprised when he didn't find one.

'Is he dead?' Nicki said beside him, her hand to her mouth as she shook.

'Yes,' Danny said, standing and giving her a hug. 'That's the strangest thing I've ever—'

A screech of tyres and a revving engine cut Danny's sentence short. He instinctively pulled Nicki in through the shop door behind them as a car sped out of the side road opposite. While tumbling into shocked customers morbidly curious at the sight of a man falling from the balcony, Danny locked eyes with the driver of the car. The same vacant expression was on his face as the man who jumped, no hint of madness or fear as he mounted the pavement and slammed the car into the pillar between the shop door and its display window. The view of the driver disappeared behind smoke, dust and exploding airbags as the display window imploded, showering them with glass crystals. Moving before the dust had settled, Danny went out the door as it swung at forty-five degrees on the bottom hinge. It took him three yanks before the car door would open. When it did, a young man around nineteen blinked away tears while holding his nose, trying to stem its bleeding.

'I, I don't know what happened. Is everyone alright? I don't understand. I was driving, er, the phone rang and then I'm here,' he said, his eyes looking normal on his confused face.

'Just stay still, buddy,' Danny said, picking up the guy's phone in the footwell. Danny and Nicki's faces looked back at him on its screen. The text above the pictures read, *New orders from command. Kill the enemy to level up.*

As Danny looked at it, the word *Deleting* appeared with a little spinning egg timer. Half a second later it—and the message—disappeared. Dropping the phone, Danny turned and went back into the shop.

'Someone call an ambulance for the driver,' he said, grabbing Nicki's hand and leading her out of the shop. 'We've gotta go. Now.'

CHAPTER 16

'A washing machine? You've gotta give this guy marks for originality,' said Theo, smiling at the CCTV picture displayed on the centre screen of the control room.

'Er, what's he doing now? Oh, is he? Yes, he's going for a death dive. Jesus, look at the size of him, he's got to be two hundred and fifty pounds,' said Phil, wincing at the shot of the drone slapping onto the pavement at Danny and Nicki's feet.

'Whoa, he hit the floor harder than you did at the Christmas party, Brian. Shame he missed the target,' said Theo, disappointed.

'At least I got back up again. I've got another drone for you, boss, incoming in twenty seconds,' said Brian from the desk behind them.

All faces turned back to the monitor as a car entered the screen at speed, its size obscuring the image of Danny and Nicki as it mounted the pavement and drove over the body on the pavement before jolting to a stop as it hit the shop front.

'Did we get them? We must have got them. Can we get anything off the camera in the driver's phone?' said Theo, straining to see past the car and debris and dust.

A picture appeared on the main screens from the driver's phone, looking up at the driver and the roof of the car above him.

'I think it's fallen into the footwell, boss,' said Phil

'Yes, I can see that, Phil. Hang on, who's that?' said Theo, seeing Danny emerge from the store and open the car door. 'Audio, Phil! Get me audio on that phone now.'

Phil tapped a few keys, and the audio came over the speakers.

"I, I don't know what happened. Is everyone alright? I don't understand. I was driving, er, the phone rang and then I'm here."

"Just stay still, buddy."

Both Theo and Kyle took half a step back in surprise as Danny's face filled the feed from the phone.

'Kill the phone feed. Now, Phil. Delete the command, quickly,' said Theo, the smile gone from his face.

'Did we at least get the girl?' said Kyle, his question answered by the CCTV feed showing Danny pulling her out of the shop and the two of them heading off down the road.

'Keep sharp, people, let's keep visual and get me more drones,' Theo said, addressing everyone in the room.

Where are you going?

'Phil, put a map up, their current location and the Miller girl's car.'

'Yes boss.'

Theo watched for a minute as their location dot moved in the direction of the parked car.

'They're going for the car. I want drones there now,' said Theo, the smile returning to his face.

CHAPTER 17

'Danny, wait, what's going on?' said Nicki, pulling against his grip on her hand until he stopped.

Danny's head whipped back. His face as hard as granite, he looked straight past Nicki, his eyes alert as they darted around, scanning the surrounding people going about their daily business.

'We've got to go,' he said without looking down at her.

'No. Tell me what happened back there,' she said, refusing to move.

Danny looked down at her. After a couple of seconds, his face softened a little. 'They were trying to kill us, the men back there. I don't know how, but I think they were being controlled. The guy in the car had our pictures and a command to kill us on his phone. It deleted as I looked at it and the driver had no idea who I was or how he got there.'

'What? But you can't control people, that's ridiculous. What was on his phone?' she said, spilling out the questions filling her head.

'I know, it sounds ridiculous, but both of them looked the same, their pupils big and a vacant look on their faces, like they were in a dream state or something. The driver's phone said, 'New orders from command, kill the enemy to level up',' said Danny, looking away to scan the street again.

'Oh my god, that can't be right.'

'What?' Danny said, looking back down at her.

'That's the same command as the game. I wrote that in the game.'

'What, Nicki, I don't understand. What are you talking about?' Danny said, confused.

'The game, the fucking game I work on at Blazer Games, Command to Kill, that's the same wording as the game. I wrote the fucking code for those commands,' Nicki said, suddenly feeling very unsafe on the street.

'Come on, we need to get out of here, get Scott, and get somewhere safe,' Danny said, setting off towards the multi-storey car park and Nicki's car.

They entered the foyer. Danny turned his back to Nicki to watch people coming and going while she paid at the ticket machine. Danny tensed when the lift to his left dinged, signalling its arrival. He breathed a sigh as the doors opened and the front of a buggy being pushed by a young mum emerged. She smiled politely and headed for the exit, rummaging in the bag hung over the handlebars for her ringing phone.

'That's it. Let's go. Lift?' Nicki said behind him.

'Er, no, let's take the stairs,' Danny said, turning towards her, not wanting to get into his aversion to lifts and their potential to get you trapped in a kill zone with no way out.

Somewhere in his subconscious, it registered that he could still hear the woman's child giggling behind him.

She didn't leave.

Before he could turn, the woman leapt on his back,

wrapping her legs around his middle while winding some strong, stretchy material around his neck, pulling it tight with surprising strength. Danny's fight instinct kicked in. He charged backwards, slamming the woman into the toughened glass panel next to the entrance doors with a boom that started the child crying. Instead of letting go, the woman pulled the pair of tights she'd taken from her bag tighter around his neck. With his face going beetroot, Danny staggered forward before falling on his back like a felled tree, trapping the woman between him and the floor. Pulling his head up, Danny powered it back in a reverse headbutt. When the grip didn't loosen, he repeated the action, feeling the crunch of the woman's nose giving way and the tights around his neck slackening off. Sitting up, he unwound the tights off his neck and sucked in great gulps of air.

Getting to his feet, Danny turned to see the pupils in the woman's watery eyes shrink back to normal, followed by a look of confusion and pain from her busted nose. Grabbing Nicki's hand, Danny headed through the door to the stairs, leaving the mother shrieking and her child crying behind them.

'Are you alright?' said Nicki, struggling to keep up with Danny as he took the stairs three at a time.

'I'll live, let's just get to the— Get back!' Danny shouted, ducking to one side as a workman complete with tool belt and hard hat jumped down the stairs swinging a hammer at his head. Ducking under the hammer's path, Danny powered two lightning punches to the man's ribs, finishing with a powerful left hook to his temple, sending the man flying down the stairs to land awkwardly on the landing below. Picking the dropped hammer off the stairs, Danny looked back at the guy. He was attempting to get up and come after them despite his leg pointing out at a right angle from a break just above the ankle. He stared without expression, his pupils unnaturally large, making his eyes look inky black.

'Should we help him?' said Nicki, wincing at the sight of his broken leg.

'No, he's still under. He'd only try to kill us. It's a busy place. He'll either come out of it and call for help or somebody will find him. Come on, let's go,' said Danny, moving up past the door to the second floor.

It swung open a second later, cutting Nicki off on the stairs below and Danny on the stairs above. Turning fast, Danny bent his legs, ready to leap on an attacker with the hammer held tightly in his hand. An old man entered the stairwell. He looked up at Danny and froze. At the same time, the workman on the landing below screamed in pain.

'My leg, aargh. Someone help me.'

'Get back, Madge,' said the old man to his wife, his eyes still fixed on Danny.

'What's that, Ernie? Move out of the way and let me through,' came his wife's nagging voice from just behind him.

'Don't argue with me, woman, get back to the car,' he shouted, backing out the door without taking an eye off Danny.

When the door closed shut, Nicki moved up and followed Danny up towards her car on the fifth floor.

'Well, that was disappointing. Who picked the yoga mum and Bob the Builder?,' said Theo, watching the CCTV feed from the stairwell camera.

'Brian,' said Kyle, looking with everyone else at Brian as he tried to shrink behind his monitor.

'Don't worry, boss, I've got something special lined up,' said Phil.

'Really, Phil, do share with the class,' said Theo, pointing to the main screens.

A few seconds later, three drone profiles appeared in front of him.

'Well, well, well, that's more like it. I hope you're paying attention, Brian,' said Theo, smiling as he read the profiles in front of him.

Phil turned towards Brian, giving him a smug smile across the room.

'Tosser,' Brian mumbled to himself while sticking his middle finger up at Phil.

CHAPTER 18

'Wait,' Danny said, holding his hand up to Nicki as they reached the door to the fifth floor parking area.

She stood back as he looked through the glass. It all looked clear, so Danny pulled the door open and stuck his head inside.

'Ok,' he said, waving Nicki through the door.

Taking the lead again, Danny moved to the rear of a van parked near the door. He looked round it towards Nicki's pickup. The floor seemed quiet, so he moved out. As Nicki followed him past the back of the van, its doors flew open and a gorilla of a man jumped down. The rear of the van went up half a foot as his weight on its springs released. Nicki turned, looking up in surprise at the sheer size of the man. He shot two shovel-sized hands out, grabbing Nicki by the neck and lifting her up off her feet to match his seven-foot height. She punched his tree trunk arms without effect, his vice-like grip and the haunting, blank look on his face driving panic into her heart.

In a flash, Danny appeared to one side and whacked

the guy on the shoulder with the hammer. He hardly moved as the blow bounced off solid muscle. Danny whacked him again. Without a sound or change of expression, the guy hurled Nicki like a ragdoll into the car beside them and turned his attention on him.

Oh, shit.

Danny swung the hammer in for a third blow, but the mountain of a man moved fast. He caught the neck of the hammer and yanked it out of Danny's grip, hurling it to one side before closing in on him. Falling back to his boxing days, Danny attacked the way you would when facing a larger opponent in the ring. He moved fast, getting underneath the mountain of a man's long reach, powering combinations of punches to the guy's rock-hard abdomen and ribs. The first few had no effect and felt like punching bags of cement. Danny kept the assault going until the guy couldn't tense his muscle against the barrage any longer and the wind went out of him.

Taking full advantage of the chink in his armour, Danny put all his body weight into an uppercut connecting under the guy's chin. The guys head flipped backward and his body followed as he fell with a boom into the back of the van he'd emerged from.

Shaking his bruised fist, Danny turned to see Nicki getting up slowly beside the car she'd been thrown into. He was just about to ask her if she was ok, when a woman in gym kit and a hoodie leapt onto the car bonnet and lashed out with a lightning kick to the side of Nicki's head, knocking her down again. In a flash, she did a spinning back flip to land prone in front of Danny.

'This is really starting to piss me off,' Danny grumbled as he adjusted his stance, ready to use the Krav Maga style of fighting he'd learned in the SAS.

The woman came at him fast with a blistering array of

karate kicks and spins, her blank face and vacant eyes making it hard to anticipate her next move. Danny blocked and countered, knocking her back a couple of steps with a knee to her side.

Damn she's quick.

She pulled off the hoodie and muttered to herself. In her mind she was battling the end of level enemy. Danny rolled his eyes at the Sydney International Karate Champion 2020 T-shirt she had on underneath it.

Of course she is, why wouldn't she be?

She came at him again even faster. He tried to block and return blows, but she was far too fast, landing kicks to his ribs and blows to his head and neck. With the wind knocked out of him, Danny went down on one knee. He tried to keep his hands up to block more blows, but the woman kicked through them with a powerful blow to his temple. As the car park started to spin around him, Danny could see her lining up for another attack, and he resigned himself to the fact that she would probably knock him out this time. Her body arched back, and she fell in a heap on the floor. Nicki stood in her place, shaking, with the hammer in her hand.

'Oh god, I haven't killed her have I?' she said, putting a hand to her mouth.

'No, she's still breathing. But if you give me that hammer, I'll bloody well finish her off,' Danny said with as much humour as he could muster while rubbing his head and slowly standing up.

'Are you alright?' she said, dropping the hammer to move by his side.

'Yeah, nothing that a long hot bath and a beer wouldn't sort out. What about you?' Danny said, looking at the red mark on her throat and the bruise already forming on the side of her face.

'I'm ok, I might join you in that bath and beer though,' she said with a smile that immediately dropped when the side of her face hurt too much.

'Er, right? Come on, let's get the fuck out of here,' Danny said awkwardly, not sure whether or not Nicki was joking about the bath.

They moved towards Nicki's pickup as fast as they could, Danny constantly checking between the parked vehicles for any more attackers.

'I'll drive,' Danny said when they reached the Ford Ranger.

'Ok, go easy on the gas when you start it or it'll flood,' Nicki said, handing him the keys.

Danny just nodded and climbed in. He turned the key, and the engine turned lazily over, failing to start after ten seconds.

'Come on, come on,' muttered Danny, turning the key again.

He was just about to click off when the engine fired up with a puff of black diesel smoke coughing out of the exhaust. He drove down through the floors as fast as he could, eager to put some distance between them and the car park as quickly as possible. They swung off the down ramp onto the ground floor and headed towards the exit, only to find the strobing blue lights from a police motorcycle reflecting off the concrete ceiling as it sat blocking the exit. The officer got off and stood in front of the bike, his visor up, eyes hidden by dark glasses. Danny stopped thirty metres short.

'Why don't we just tell the police?' Nicki said, looking across to Danny.

He didn't answer her straight away. The hairs on the back of his neck prickled and a voice in his head was telling him this was wrong.

'He's one of them,' Danny finally said, slamming the pickup into gear and flooring it.

At the same time, the officer drew his handgun and started firing in their direction.

'Get down,' shouted Danny, sliding down in the seat.

Nicki flopped down below the window as a bullet punched a hole through the front window, ripping through the headrest above her head before exiting out the rear window. Picking up speed, Danny yanked the steering wheel to one side, bounced up off the kerb and crashing the pickup through the barrier of the entrance lane to the car park as bullets took out the side windows, showering them in glass crystals.

The police officer followed the pickup as it flew out onto the street, firing his gun until the clip clicked empty. He calmly ejected the magazine and loaded a full one before getting back on his bike. Revving it up, he spun the bike around in a tight circle, smoke pouring off the tyre until it gripped the tarmac, sending the bike speeding out of the car park after them.

CHAPTER 19

Deep inside the Blink Defence Systems building, Theo's calm facade fell as he watched Danny slide sideways out of the car park and disappear down the street. He grabbed the monitor off the desk beside him and heaved it upward, bending and ripping all the connecting cables before smashing it on the floor with all his might. 'Goddamn it, what do I have to do to kill this guy?' he shouted, before pushing his hair back with his fingers and taking a few deep breaths to compose himself.

The room fell silent at the outburst. Nobody wanted to be the first to speak.

'Delete the last twenty minutes of camera feeds from the car park's CCTV, and fill the gap with a loop from earlier. Don't forget to add a new timestamp,' said Theo, calm and upbeat again as if nothing had happened.

'Yes boss, already on it,' said Brian, eager to score points against Phil.

'Good. Take care of the drone's phone data as well. Phil, find out where they are going.'

'Yes boss, they're heading north, possibly going for the

Harbour Bridge. We've still got a drone in pursuit, the motorcycle cop.'

'Well, at least that's something. Get me a camera feed and some more drones. Oh, and can someone clean this crap up?' Theo said, pointing to the smashed up monitor while casting an eye to Jeff at the back of the room.

'Yes boss, right away,' he said, jumping out of his seat.

'Shall I call Maaka?' Kyle said, leaning over to speak quietly.

Theo thought for a minute. This was not going the way he'd expected it to.

'Call him, tell him to get his men ready. Just in case,' Theo whispered back.

Kyle nodded and quietly left the room with his phone to his ear.

CHAPTER 20

'He's catching up,' said Nicki over the wind and traffic noise through the glassless windows.

'Yeah I see him,' Danny said, looking in the rear view mirror.

The powerful police bike cut easily through the traffic as it got ever closer. When it got within a few car lengths, the rider pulled his handgun out and started firing again.

'For fuck's sake,' growled Danny, the rear view mirror exploding with the impact of a bullet as he took another look at the closing bike. 'Right, I've had enough of this prick, hold on tight.'

Danny stamped his foot on the brake and yanked the handbrake up at the same time, smoke pouring off the front tyres as they locked up, while the back tyres juddered and bounced on the tarmac. The front of the bike dipped sharply as the police officer pulled on the brakes as hard as he could, but the bike was travelling too fast and hit the tailgate of the pickup with a sickening metallic thud. The officer was thrown forward, his legs hitting the handlebars as the rear wheel lifted off the ground, sending the gun clattering into the back of the pickup and the officer somersaulting into the back of the cab before flopping motionless into a heap. Danny wanted to climb in the back and throw him out, but the crash was already attracting a lot of attention from traffic and city-goers around them.

'I'll deal with him in a minute, first we need to get away from here, find Scott and ditch this vehicle,' Danny said, crunching the pickup into gear and driving off, leaving the police motorbike bent and on its side in the road.

'But where is Scott?' said Nicki, looking out the rear window at the crowd of people congregating around the wrecked motorcycle.

'He said the MacIntyre lot were taking him to lunch at a restaurant in the Opera House, Benny's or something like that.'

'Bennelong restaurant.'

'Yeah that was it,' Danny said, slowing a little as he tried not to draw any more attention to himself.

'Take the next right, it's not far from here.'

Danny did as Nicki said, emerging out from between the tall city centre buildings as he drove along Park Street with Hyde Park on either side.

'Turn left there, at the other side of the park,' Nicki said.

Danny had to give her credit, she was holding together well; most people would be a gibbering wreck by now. They followed the road along the park, stopping alongside a cement lorry at the traffic lights at the top of the park. Anxious at stopping with an unconscious police officer in the back of the pickup, Danny drummed his fingers on the steering wheel while he scanned the people and cars turning across the junction. The traffic camera on the opposite side of the junction caught his eye and got his mind thinking.

How did they know where we were all the time? They must have tracked us through CCTV and traffic cameras.

Putting the pickup into first, ready to pull away, Danny glanced across to see the driver of the cement truck bringing his phone up to his ear. Two seconds later he looked at the screen and turned his head in their direction. Large, dark eyes locked on them out of an expressionless face. The big diesel engine revved, blowing puffs of smoke out of the steel exhaust pipes running up the back of the truck's cab.

'Time to go,' Danny said, yanking the steering wheel to go around the stationary car ahead of them and cut through the red light.

The driver of the cement truck dumped it into gear, lurching it forward into the car in front, smashing it out of the way as though it was a dinky toy.

'Shit, he's coming, go up there,' Nicki shouted, pointing up Macquarie Street.

Turning in her seat to watch the truck out of the rear window, Nicki saw the back of the policeman's crash helmet pop into view as he sat up in the back of the pickup. He slid the helmet off and shook his head, dazed, as he tried to figure out where he was and what had happened.

'Danny.'

'What?' said Danny looking at the temperature gauge going through the roof on the dash and a trail of steam floating over the bonnet from a bullet hole in the radiator.

'The policeman's awake!' she shouted, watching him turn to face them, thankful to see his pupils not large, but normal.

'Is he trying to kill us?' Danny yelled over the noise.

'I don't think so.'

'Well that's a first. Fuck him, I'm more worried about the fifty-tonne cement truck on our ass at the moment.'

'Sir, I need you to pull the vehicle over now,' the police officer shouted through the glassless rear window.

'Sorry, can't do,' Danny yelled back, sending the police officer rolling to one side, as he swerved to overtake a slow moving car. Seconds later there was a loud metallic crunching sound as the cement truck struck the back of the same car, pushing it off the road and into the front of an office building.

The officer looked from the truck to Danny and then back again, totally at a loss as to what was going on. He reached for his gun, only to feel the empty holster. Spinning around, he spotted it at the back of the flat bed area he was in. Sliding across, he grabbed it and turned back, pointing it at the back of Danny's head.

'Stop this vehicle now. I won't tell you again,' he shouted.

'Listen, dickhead, for your information, we just saved your ass when that maniac in the cement truck tried to kill you after you gave him a ticket, and, if you hadn't noticed, he's pretty determined to finish the job. So if you really want to shoot someone, shoot him, ok?' Danny shouted back, just as the engine started knocking loudly and black smoke trailed out of the exhaust.

The officer paused, frustrated. The last thing he could remember, he was heading back to the station to finish his shift. The cement truck bashing the back of the pickup made his mind up. Spinning around, he aimed his gun at the truck tyres. The third bullet found its target, blowing out the front offside tyre which caused the cement truck to turn sharply. It jack-knifed and slid down the road, obliterating parked cars and a small tree before it came to a stop in a cloud of dust. Danny pulled the clattering pickup to a stop and let the officer hop down onto the tarmac.

'Stay here,' the officer said, walking cautiously towards the truck.

'Yes sir,' Danny said, waiting until he'd taken ten paces towards the truck before he stamped on the gas and took off down the street in a cloud of black smoke.

CHAPTER 21

'Theo, shut it down. All this destruction across the city is going to raise too many questions. Get Maaka to deal with them, quietly,' said Kyle, frowning at the carnage on the screens.

Theo stared intently at the traffic camera feed showing Nicki's pickup smoking off up the road. He didn't move for half a minute until he finally turned and spoke. 'Shut it down and clean up,' he bellowed to the room before turning to Kyle. 'Tell Maaka to get it done, whatever it takes,' he said quietly before leaving the room.

Kyle pressed a number on his phone and put it to his ear. 'You've got a green light, whatever it takes,' he said before hanging up.

Danny limped the pickup under the flyover on the approach road to the Opera House. He coasted around the roundabout at the top and rolled down the ramp to the underground car park for the Opera House. He parked the pickup in the nearest free space and got out. Nicki moved around to his side and the two of them exited, walking along the pedestrian walkway with all the tourists heading towards the famous Opera House. Nicki grabbed Danny's hand as they walked, taking him by surprise.

'To blend in,' she said with a smile when he looked puzzled.

'Yeah, good idea,' he said back, trying not to think about how attractive she looked.

'That's the Bennelong restaurant,' Nicki said, pointing to the smaller of the iconic shaped buildings as they climbed the steps to the entrance doors. They walked through the foyer and into the very upmarket Bennelong restaurant, where the maître d' stood looking unimpressed by the two disheveled people in front of him.

'Good afternoon, sir, madam. Can I help you?'

'Yes, I have an urgent message for one of the MacIntyre party,' Danny said, trying to see Scott in the restaurant.

'Certainly, sir. If you would like to follow me, I will escort you to their table,' the maître d' said, turning to lead him.

'Er, no, sorry, could you just tell Mr Miller his security consultant needs a word?' said Danny, fishing a note out of his pocket and handing it folded to the maître d'.

'Of course, sir, thank you, sir, you're, er, too kind,' he said, the smile falling from his face when he saw a paltry five dollar note in his hand.

A few moments later, he returned with Scott following closely behind.

'Daniel, what on earth are you doing here, and why are

you holding my sister's hand?' Scott said, looking from one to the other.

'Er, we were just blending in,' said Danny, releasing Nicki's hand as if it was on fire. 'Anyway, forget that. Look, none of us are safe. We've gotta get out of here, out of the city, now, mate.'

'Unsafe, how? Would you care to elaborate, dear boy?' Scott said.

'Look, we haven't got time, bruv, people are trying to kill us,' said Nicki impatiently.

'Ok, I'll go and make my excuses. Where's the car?'

'The car's dead. We've gotta find some transport,' Danny said bluntly.

'Yeah, a police officer shot it, then a lorry drove into us,' added Nicki.

'Of course they did. Why am I not surprised?' muttered Scott, heading back to the MacIntyre table.

'Gentlemen, I'm afraid I must leave you. I have a matter of national security I have to deal with—the UK's, not yours,' Scott said with a smile.

'Of course, Mr Miller, I totally understand. If there's anything we can do…' said the CEO of the MacIntyre group.

'Well, now you mention it, old boy, there is something you could help me out with,' Scott said, shaking hands around the table as he prepared to leave.

Danny and Nicki watched Scott as he returned. When he reached them, he reached out a hand and dangled a car key in front of Danny.

'Try not to damage it, you caveman. I would very much like to return it in one piece,' he said with a smile.

'Nice one, Scotty boy.'

'Now, would somebody kindly tell me what's going on?' Scott said, following them out the exit.

COMMAND TO KILL

They filled Scott in on the way to the car, the attackers, the phone commands like the game commands Nicki programmed for Command to Kill, and how their attackers seemed to track them through the city.

'Mmm, yes, I'm inclined to agree with you about getting out of the city. If Theo Blazer and Blink Defence Systems are behind this, he certainly has the capability to access government, traffic and domestic cameras, and track us with facial recognition software. The big question is, if we get out of the city where will we go? It needs to be somewhere off the beaten track, no traffic cameras or CCTV, the more remote the better,' said Scott, sitting in the back of the loaned MacIntyre limousine.

'As it happens, I have just the place,' Nicki said, smiling.

'Good, I need to pick up my laptop and phone from yours first,' Scott said to Nicki.

'Yeah and I need to pick up the satellite phone Simon sent. We'll have to be quick, if the police track Nicki's pickup, they'll be round to ask questions soon enough,' said Danny, driving carefully past the overturned cement truck, surrounded by four police cars and an ambulance with their lights flashing.

'More of your handiwork, I presume,' said Scott.

CHAPTER 22

Maaka watched from behind the blacked-out windows of the Toyota Land Cruiser as Jedda and Atama returned from scouting Nicki's house out and climbed in the back.

'They left about forty minutes ago,' said Jedda.

'Hey, Abo, how do you know that? You lick the door knob or sniff a blade of grass?' said Karl, looking back from the front seat, grinning.

'Call me Abo one more time, Karl, and I'll put a bullet in your head.'

'Oi, knock it off,' growled Maaka, silencing the two of them. 'What did you find out, Jedda?'

'A neighbour saw them leave, said they looked like they were in a hurry, they left in a large, black, Audi saloon car,' said Jedda, still staring Karl in the eye, both men refusing to be the first one to turn away.

'I said knock it off, you two,' growled Maaka, placing his phone to his ear. 'Kyle, we missed them. Do a camera search for a large, black, Audi saloon. It left the area approximately forty minutes ago.'

'Ok, you'd better leave. The police found Miller's Ford Ranger in a carpark next to the Opera House. They've dispatched a unit to check out her home address. Keep mobile, we'll let you know as soon as we get a lead,' said Kyle, walking between Phil and Brian as they scoured camera feeds for a glimpse of Danny, Nicki or Scott and a large, black Audi saloon car.

Maaka hung up without answering. 'Let's go,' he said to Karl.

They pulled smoothly away, driving past Nicki's house, turning at the end of the street as a police patrol car passed them on the other side.

'Oh god, I've died and gone to hell,' said Scott, following Danny and Nicki into an Aldi supermarket just off the motorway north of Sydney.

'Shut up, you posh prick,' said Danny, grabbing a basket.

'Seriously, don't they have a Waitrose or M&S here?' said Scott, turning his nose up at the stacked up toilet rolls just inside the store.

'How the hell did my brother turn into such a dick?' said Nicki, walking away from him to catch up with Danny.

'Charming, with friends like you two, who needs enemies?' Scott mumbled to himself.

They got food and provisions to last a few days. Despite his protest, Scott ended up filling half the basket, which made Danny and Nicki chuckle. They paid and left Mount Kuring, getting back onto the motorway, and continued to head away from Sydney. The journey dragged on mile after mile until towns and civilisation were replaced by rolling countryside and rocky mountains.

'How much further is this place? We've been driving for over two hours,' complained Scott from the back of the Audi.

'About another forty minutes,' said Nicki, taking a peek at the sat nav as she drove.

'You sure about this place, sis?'

'Yeah, I've only been there once. It's really remote, the nearest neighbour's about three miles away. No brainwashed crowds to try and kill us, and no CCTV to track us. It was my ex's grandparents' place. It's been empty since they passed away. The lazy shit was supposed to do it up and sell it, but he was always too busy drinking or gambling my money away to be bothered.'

'I'm sorry I wasn't there for you,' Scott said, putting a hand on her shoulder.

'Don't worry about it. That chapter of my life is well and truly over, and this one is far scarier. How are you so calm?'

'Because we have something they don't,' said Scott, sitting back.

'Yeah, and what's that?' said Nicki, looking confused in the rear-view mirror at him.

'Him,' Scott said, looking across at Danny sleeping in the passenger seat.

'How can he sleep with all that's going on?' Nicki said, shaking her head.

'Ah, if he were awake he'd quote you one of his Special Forces mottos. Eat and sleep when you can, because you never know when you'll get the next chance,' said Scott, mimicking Danny.

'Mmm, he is a force of nature,' Nicki said, looking across at Danny.

'That he is, my dear, but let me warn you, love and relationships have never ended well for Daniel or his partners.'

'Huh, what, why do you say that?' Nicki said, suddenly defensive.

'I'm not blind, Nichola. I've seen the way you look at him and the way he looks at you.'

'Rubbish, and don't call me Nichola. Dad was the only one who called me Nichola,' said Nicki, a tear forming in her eye.

'Sorry, Nicki. I'm just saying be careful. You and Daniel are the most important people in my life and I wouldn't want to see either of you hurt,' said Scott, patting his sister on the shoulder again.

Wiping the tear from her eye, Nicki drove on in silence.

Danny woke up as the road got more remote and bumpy.

'Afternoon, sleepyhead,' said Nicki.

'Where are we?'

'McCullys Gap, the farmhouse is a couple of miles outside town.'

'This is a town?' Danny said, looking at the odd farmhouse at the end of long dirt tracks tailing off from either side of the road.

'It is around here,' Nicky answered.

'Good, until I can figure the best course of action, the quieter the better.'

Fifteen minutes later, Nicki turned off the road onto an overgrown track. They rumbled and bounced along uphill for two miles before driving up to a large, tin-clad, two-storey house beside two massive water silos and a tin-structured barn. Looking beyond the buildings, a vast savannah of tree-dotted grasslands fell away for miles, with tree-covered rocky mountains lining the horizon beyond. The nearest farm building was barely visible in the distance.

'Perfect,' Danny said, doing a three-sixty-degree turn, approving of the high ground position of the house and the impossibility of attack without a two mile warning.

CHAPTER 23

After popping a hole in the glass, Danny reached in, unlocked the back door, and walked into the kitchen. The whole building had an old, self-built feel about it, and the dated, brown formica kitchen was no exception. He clicked a light switch and a harsh strip light blinked into life.

At least the power's still on. Scott's going to love this.

Bang on cue, Scott came in carrying the groceries. 'Good grief, it's worse than I thought. Take me back to Sydney, I'd rather take my chances with the psycho brain-washed killers,' he said, running a finger along the dust covered kitchen worktop, eyeing it disapprovingly.

'Shut up, you big idiot,' said Nicki, following him in.

'I've got to make a call,' Danny said, pausing to look at a thin metal gun cabinet bolted to the wall by the coat rack before walking outside.

He fetched the sat phone out of the car and powered it up. When it eventually got satellite lock Danny hit one on the speed dial.

'Mr Pearson, I've been expecting your call,' came Simon's smooth, university-educated voice.

'Why?' Danny said bluntly.

'Ah, well, when a trail of madness with no logical explanation hits Sydney, enquiring minds begin to wonder. Especially when surviving parties have no recollection as to what happened. One could be forgiven for thinking they had been controlled, like drone soldiers perhaps.'

'So what are we going to do about it?' asked Danny.

'We? Why would I do anything about it? It would seem to me to be your problem,' replied Simon, jovial as ever.

'Cut the crap, Simon, Neither you, Russia, China or anyone else can afford to have this kind of weapon controlled by any one country. Someone's got to take him down.'

'Mmm, true, but our friend Theodore Blazer is virtually a national hero. He has connections everywhere, and with the small fortune he contributes to the Liberal Party, we are unlikely to get any support from the government without a substantial amount of proof.'

'So what do we do?' Danny said, not disguising the irritation in his voice.

'Mr Blazer wrote the book on intelligence systems. He's likely been tracking you through phones, card payments and every camera feed you can think of. So firstly, I'd get out of the city, go remote and—'

'Already ahead of you,' Danny said, interrupting Simon.

'I thought you would be. Blazer has a supercomputer called Hercules at Blink Defence Systems. He also hosts all Blink's programs and data on his own servers from inside Blink Defence Systems.'

'And this helps me how?'

'Let me see, if only you had a world renowned

computer expert on hand to figure out a way of getting the drone program files out of Hercules to prove it exists,' Simon said sarcastically.

'Or I could just kill Blazer,' Danny said in a low growl.

'Yes you could, but I'm not sure that would be the end of it. Blink was set up many years ago by Theodore Blazer's father. It's a large corporation with a board of directors and shareholders. Killing the figurehead would not kill the company. Blazer's right-hand man, Kyle Drago, would become acting CEO and then it's business as usual.'

'Get the program files it is then,' said Danny, as if it were as easy as popping down the shops.

'I admire your optimism, Mr Pearson. Although my hands are tied for now, a contact tells me there is discord in the American camp that has been financing the project. I've also been in contact with a colleague in the Australian security council. You get me the drone program, and I'll make sure Theodore Blazer and Blink Defence Systems are shut down for good,' said Simon, his jovial tone turning more serious.

'I'll be in touch,' was all Danny said.

'Oh, and Mr Pearson?'

'What?'

'As I'm sure you're aware, if this all goes pear-shaped, Her Majesty's government will deny any knowledge of you or our conversation. You'll be on your own,' Simon finished bluntly.

'I always am,' said Danny gruffly, before hanging up.

He paced around outside the farmhouse in the red glow of the sinking sun, his mind ticking through what Simon had said. Walking behind the water tanks, Danny turned his attention to the tin sheet covered barn, with its heavy chain and padlock securing the doors. He rattled it before examining the door hinges and panelled front.

Leaving it, Danny went around the side to a pile of old fence posts, metal sheets, and rusty farm equipment. It had been there a long time by the looks of the weeds and long grass growing through all the gaps. Spotting the end of a metal bar poking out from under a metal sheet, Danny grabbed the end and lifted the sheet to one side. A coiled-up snake powered a strike at him with lightning speed. Danny barely had time to move, and ended up pulling the bar out as he fell back on his arse, dropping the sheet on top of the snake as its bite fell millimetres short and it recoiled back out of sight.

Getting up, Danny wiped the cold sweat from his forehead and cast his mind back to Special Forces training in indigenous snakes. He was fairly sure it was either a death adder or an eastern tiger snake. Either way, it was one of the most venomous in the world and you didn't want to get bitten by it out here.

With his breathing returning to normal, he took the metal bar back to the barn and shoved it under the hinged side of one of the locked doors. Raising the long bar up, Danny squatted and hooked it on his shoulder, lifting with all his might. The hinges inched up with a squeaky protest until they popped off the pin holding them in place. The door flopped forward, its top flapping about as the bottom dug in the dirt, leaving a gap to enter. Dropping the bar, Danny went inside and flicked on the light. A smile crossed his face as he eyed up the workbench with a set of long range radios and tools hanging along the back wall. The other side of the barn had fencing supplies, fertiliser, jerry cans of fuel and an assortment of farm equipment including an old tractor and trailer.

Mmm, very useful.

Looking outside at the fading light, Danny grabbed a

crowbar off the bench, flicked off the light, and headed back into the farmhouse.

'You've been a while. What was the outcome of the phone call?' said Scott, sitting at the kitchen table with a beer.

'Oh, the usual. No one's coming to help us. You've got to hack into Blink's super computer and steal the drone program, while I stop us all getting killed,' Danny said, jamming the point of the crowbar into the door crack of the metal gun cabinet, and pulling it with a quick jolt.

The side of the cabinet bent outwards and the door popped open to expose a bolt-action hunting rifle and an open box of ammunition with six bullets in.

'Is that all? Thank goodness for that. For a minute there, I thought we were in trouble,' said Scott with a grin that made Danny laugh.

'Where's Nicki?'

'She's just freshening up. What have you found in there?' said Scott.

'Something to even up the odds. Don't go wandering too far from the house,' said Danny, turning serious.

'Why, do you think they'll find us here?' said Scott.

'Given enough time and resources, you can find anyone anywhere. Blazer's not short on resources, so time's the only unknown factor,' said Danny, raising his beer to Scott before taking a big swig.

CHAPTER 24

Theo roughly dried his hair with a towel after his shower. It was only 8:30a.m. but the surf on Bondi Beach below his penthouse apartment had been up this morning, and he'd been out there making the most of it since six. He padded through to his kitchen and made himself a coffee before sitting on the terrace to watch the other surfers as he drank. His mobile rang, ruining the moment and turning his face into a frown.

'Yes.'

'We've got a hit on Scott Miller's credit card,' came Kyle's voice over the phone.

'Hang on,' said Theo, getting up and moving to his office.

He placed his hand on the palm reader and sat in his $18,000 office chair, commissioned from designer Hans J. Wegner. The six screens mounted around him burst into life.

'Go on,' Theo commanded, switching the phone to speaker as he scrolled through Hercules' files and shared screens.

'Scott Miller used his card to pay for groceries at an Aldi store in Mount Kuring yesterday afternoon,' said Kyle.

'CCTV?'

'On screen one now,' said Kyle, indicating to Phil to put the feed up.

It appeared at the same time on Theo's top left screen. Scott, Danny and Nicki were clearly visible leaving Aldi and walking across the car park to a black Audi A8. As the car reversed out to drive off, an enhancement bubble appeared over the number plate, sharpening up the registration.

'Where did they get the car? Is it hired or stolen?'

'Neither. The car belongs to the MacIntyre Group. They are a client of Scott Miller. I had Brian call to say the vehicle had been seen running a red light. A very chatty receptionist said the vehicle was on loan to a Scott Miller after he was called away from a lunch meeting on matters of UK national security yesterday.'

'Mmm. What else have we got?'

'ANPR caught the plate as it joined the M1 to Seahampton, and again when it joined the M15 heading north until the motorway changed to the A15.'

'And then?'

'And then they keep going until Muswellbrook and disappear. We have them passing on a CCTV feed outside a pump and pipeline supplier, but they don't appear on the next traffic camera five kilometres further along the A15,' said Kyle, dragging and expanding maps on the main and shared screens.

'I see. How many exits do we have?' said Theo, more thinking out loud than asking as he studied the maps displayed on the shared screen.

'There are four or five dirt tracks that don't really lead

anywhere. The most likely route would be along Sandy Creek Road. It heads north west through the mountains. It's mostly farmland out there, plenty of remote places to lie low. I've got Phil tracking IPs for camera feeds on properties that run along the road. We've also hacked all Nicki Miller's contacts and social network files. Hercules is cross-referencing them against the property register for any addresses in the area.'

'Good. Get Maaka out there now and send him any updates you get.'

'He's already on his way,' said Kyle calmly.

'Excellent. I'll be in, in about an hour,' Theo said, hanging up. He expanded and moved the satellite map, following Sandy Creek Road as it wound past dozens of widely spaced long drives leading to dozens of remote farmhouses.

The phone ringing pulled him away from the screen, the contact ID putting a frown on his face for the second time that morning.

'General, what an unexpected pleasure. What can I do for you?' Theo said, with well practised corporate diplomacy, his silky smooth tone hiding the nervousness he had at talking to the General.

'Don't give me that unexpected pleasure horseshit. What the hell do you think you're playing at using drones—my drones—all over Sydney?' the General ordered in a loud voice.

'Your drones?'

'Yes, Blazer, my goddamn drones, paid for with goddamn US of A dollars. You might have developed this program and you might facilitate it through your command centre, but I own it, and I don't want you taking a shit unless I say so. Do you understand me?' the General continued, talking to Theo like he was tearing a strip off a cadet on the parade ground.

There was an awkward silence while Theo fought between the urge to hang up on the General and cutting him out of the deal, or take a more tactful response. The tactful response won.

'My dear General, there is no question that you have control of this project. The events of yesterday were an unfortunate necessity, brought about by a serious security breach.'

'What kind of breach are we talking about?' said the General, flipping into operational directness.

'We discovered one of my employees at Blazer Games is working for British intelligence, and with the help of two additional agents, was trying to infiltrate Blink Defence's drone project,' said Theo, getting back into his stride.

'I see, and that situation is now resolved?'

'Absolutely, General. The project worked perfectly, no evidence and no comeback from the authorities. The targets fled the city and have taken refuge in a remote location in the hills. I have deployed my personal security team to clean up any loose ends.'

'Mmm, good. You report to me when it's done,' said the General gruffly.

'Of course, General,' said Theo, rolling his eyes, already bored with the conversation.

'And Blazer?'

'Yes, General.'

'Anything else happens, you don't act without talking to me first. Do I make myself clear?'

'Crystal clear, General,' said Theo, hanging up and chucking the phone on the desk angrily.

Arrogant American tosser, who the hell does he think he is talking to?

CHAPTER 25

'I don't trust that slippery son of a bitch as far as I can throw him,' said General Simmonds, his office looking out onto a small command centre.

'You know my views on this project,' said Agent Johnson without gloating, just a statement of fact.

'Don't you start giving me the I-told-you-so speech, Stan, we need this project. I've got twenty-two top level terrorists, dictators and political activists on my list. They're responsible for countless deaths and I can't touch them because they're pulling all the strings from politically sensitive countries. One whiff of the US taking them out and it's all out war. We need to use Blazer's drones, the barbers, the drivers, chefs, hell, I'd use their paperboy if it meant they were erased off this planet.'

'They're still innocent victims,' Johnson said, looking the General in the eyes.

'We're at war, Stan, and war comes with collateral damage.'

The room went quiet as the two men broodingly agreed to disagree.

'To hell with it,' the General said, picking up the phone and dialling an extension number. 'Henry, get me Sergeant Pace please, and get me a transport plane to Sydney as soon as possible.'

Putting the phone down he turned back to Johnson. 'We're going back to make sure Blazer doesn't screw this up. You've got contacts with London. Call them, find out what you can about these agents. I want to know whose toes I'll be stepping on if we neutralise them.'

Johnson got up and left the office without replying. His mind was spinning. The breach of humanitarian rights the project presented was bad enough, but now the General and Blazer were planning to kill agents belonging to the US's closest allies. He walked down the corridor to his office and slumped into his leather chair. Reaching for the phone, he stopped, his hand hovering above the receiver. Retracting it, he pulled his mobile out and stared at it, the fear and paranoia from working at Department 23 stopping him from using them. Leaving the office, Johnson headed down the stairs and out the officially non-existent hangar, located far away from the main buildings at Fort Bragg army base. He got into one of the parked black sedans and drove across the base to the main gate, flashing his ID to drive out. Twenty minutes later, Johnson parked up in downtown Fayetteville and headed into a diner. He ordered a coffee and a slice of apple pie, wandering across to the payphone while the waitress went to get his order.

'Hi, it's me. Our friend is out of control, we need to meet. It has to be today.'

'Why today?'

'There's trouble with the project, the English are involved. He's got us and a Delta Force team on transport to Sydney tonight.'

'Where are you?'

'Downtown Fayetteville, Sally's Diner on Gillespie Street.'

'I'll be there in twenty minutes.'

Agent Johnson sat down, the coffee and pie waiting on the table in front of him. He took a drink of his coffee while he waited, his leg bouncing up and down nervously under the table. He moved the pie around the plate with his fork, his appetite suddenly leaving him.

CHAPTER 26

'Morning, Scotty boy, Nicki, how's it going?' Danny said, walking into the kitchen and riffling through the cupboards.

'Huh, what? Can't talk right now,' said Scott without looking up from his laptop. The soft tap of his typing sounded like ten people due to the lightning speed his fingers moved.

'I wouldn't disturb him. He's well in the zone,' said Nicki, getting up from her laptop to put the kettle on.

'What's he doing? Aha,' Danny said, grinning at the pair of oven gloves he found in a drawer.

'Er, code, he's rewriting the drone program code with a new set of command triggers to replace the ones Blazer uses to control people.'

'Oh, ok, er, why?' Danny said in surprise.

'Once we've copied the program files, Scott wants to upload new commands to Hercules and send it to everyone on the database before deleting it. If Blazer doesn't know the new command, he can't control those poor people. It won't stop him for long, but it might slow him down long enough for Simon to get him shut down. The hardest part is figuring out a way to get into Blink Defence Systems and upload it to Hercules,' said Nicki, looking curiously at Danny holding a pair of oven gloves and an empty pillowcase in one hand, and a mop handle with a hook-shaped coat hanger attached in the other.

'Can't you just dial it in or something?'

'No, you need someone with administrator access to get in.'

'What, like Blazer?'

'Yes, like—Blazer! Danny, you're a genius,' said Nicki, leaning in and giving him a big kiss on the cheek.

'I am?' said Danny, puzzled.

'Yes, you are. Blazer has a big computer setup at his penthouse apartment. He threw a party there when we launched Command to Kill. I remember him bragging that he could control all of Blazer Games and Blink Defence from it.'

'Very good, my dear, but how are we going to get his login details to access it?' said Scott, lifting his head up from behind his laptop.

'Can't you just tap, tap, tap and hack it?' said Danny.

'People like Blazer have top level security. It will take considerably more than a tap, tap, tap to access his computer,' Scott said, rolling his eyes at Danny's comment.

'Hang on, he didn't use a login, his terminal opens with a palm reader like the ones at work.'

'A palm reader. How jolly modern of him. Exactly like the ones at Blazer Games?' said Scott, noticing Danny still standing by the sink with the oven gloves, a pillowcase and a mop handle.

'Yeah, the same. Why?' said Nicki, puzzled.

'Because Blazer's palm scan will have the same code across Blazer Games, Blink Defence and his home hub.

Blink Defence would be very hard to get into, but if we could sneak into Blazer Games, we could get the code for his palm print off the security computer that operates the door locks,' Scott said before turning his attention back to Danny. 'What the devil are you up to, Daniel?'

'Oh this? I need some sheets of metal from the pile by the barn. The last one I touched had teeth,' said Danny, walking out grinning as Scott and Nicki watched him go, none the wiser.

After retrieving the metal sheets, Danny carefully placed the pillowcase in an empty plastic container in the barn, making sure he snapped the lid on tight. Straining to lift the barn door already off its hinges, Danny dragged it and the door padlocked to it all the way open. Minutes later, he drove the tractor out with a trailer attached, stopping it just outside the barn. He loaded the trailer with the metal sheets, shovels, fertiliser bags, jerry cans of fuel and two large rolls of electric fence wire. Satisfied, he drove off down the long drive, stopping around four hundred metres from the house. The sound of a car engine in the distance caused Danny to stop and look up. A couple of miles down the hill, he watched as two blacked-out Toyota Land Cruisers came into view on Sandy Creek Road. The hairs on the back of Danny's neck stood up. He reached for the hunting rifle in the trailer, kneeling down to rest his elbow on the trailer, keeping the rifle rock steady as he followed the vehicles through the telescopic sight. The blacked-out glass gave no clue as to the occupants, but the shiny, clean black cars didn't look like the well-worn workhorses the farm folk around here would use.

The cars passed the turning for the farmhouse and kept on going until only the dust cloud in their wake was visible. Danny stayed motionless, his eye glued to the sight for a further five minutes until he was satisfied they weren't coming back. A little while later, he was back at the farmhouse. He'd moved the Audi out of sight around the back of the barn, and was digging twenty metres away from the house.

'What's he doing out there?' Nicki said, watching Danny digging like a man possessed in the hot sun.

'Perhaps he's digging a swimming pool,' said Scott without looking up from his laptop.

Ignoring her brother, Nicki grabbed a cold can of beer out of the fridge and went outside.

'Hey, I thought you could use one of these,' she said, handing Danny the cold can.

'Thanks.'

'What are you doing?' Nicki said, picking up a long range radio with two cables hanging out before disappearing through a wax seal on the end of a bullet casing.

'Whoa, whoa, don't press any buttons, lay that down gently please, Nicki,' said Danny, the worried look on his face panicking her a little.

'What is it?'

'It's a radio detonator.'

'Detonator for what?' Nicki said.

'Twenty-five kilos of ammonium nitrate-based fertiliser mixed with petrol and packed with nails, screws and bits of farm machinery. Boom,' said Danny, emphasising an explosion with his hands.

'Isn't that a bit extreme?' said Nicki, backing away from the trailer.

'Plan for the worst, hope for the best. Let's hope we don't need it,' Danny said, trying to reassure her.

'What else have you been up to out here?' Nicki said, wondering where she should tread.

'Just don't go wandering about too far from the house,' Danny said with a grin.

CHAPTER 27

'Yes,' said Maaka, standing back from the others, studying the map spread across the hood of the car.

'We've got a lead on the Miller girl. Her ex-husband's grandparents had a farm, Coopers Farm, near a place called McCullys Gap,' said Kyle from the command centre.

'And the grandparents?'

'Passed away. The property's been empty for the last eight months.'

'Ok, we'll check it out,' said Maaka, looking at the sun starting to dip in the late afternoon sky.

'Let me know when it's done,' said Kyle, before hanging up.

'Listen up, guys, we've got an address twenty miles back. Load up, let's go,' Maaka ordered.

Karl, Jedda and Atama got in the lead vehicle with Maaka while four other men climbed in the vehicle behind. Spinning the vehicles around, they headed in convoy back towards McCullys Gap. Half an hour later Maaka had

Karl pull up a few hundred metres short of the dirt drive up to the farmhouse. He climbed out and looked at the tiny image of the farmhouse a few miles up the hill. He reached his arm back and Jedda handed him a powerful pair of binoculars.

'Looks quiet,' said Karl, squinting against the low sun as he stood beside Maaka.

'Looks can be deceiving. There's a tractor and trailer out by the barn and a smoke trail coming out of the chimney.'

'Let's go in and finish them then,' said Karl, a glint of excitement in his eye.

'No, we wait. It'll be dark in a couple of hours. We'll go in then,' said Maaka, still scanning the farm with the binoculars.

'Fuck that, I say we go in now,' growled Karl.

'We go in when it's dark, now get back in the fucking car,' Maaka said, his voice direct as he stared, daring Karl to argue with him again.

'Ok, ok, don't know what you're worried about, it's just two geeks and a washed up soldier,' Karl grumbled as he turned back to the car.

'That washed up soldier took out a dozen drones and knew Atama was following him. Nobody ever knows Atama is following them,' said Maaka walking to the car behind, its window opening as he approached.

'What do you want us to do?' the driver said through the open window.

'You go back over the brow of the hill and wait. We'll go half a mile past the farm. If they try to leave, we've got the road covered. We go in at eight, ok?'

'Roger that, guv.'

'Where's Daniel gone now?' said Scott, turning the light on in the kitchen.

'I don't know. I saw him head off down the drive with some dirty old sheet and the rifle,' said Nicki nervously.

Four hundred metres down the drive, Danny lay flat, tucked in behind a tree in the dry grass. He had the sheet soiled with mud and grass and twigs covering him as he lay motionless, looking at Maaka and his men through the rifle scope. He watched Maaka looking at the farmhouse through the binoculars and Karl saying something before getting a ticking off and climbing back into the car. Finally, Maaka took off in the lead car, driving past the dirt road to the farm to disappear from sight where the road dipped. Swinging the scope back, Danny watched the other car turn around and head away from him.

Mmm, can't drive out. A fight it is then.

He looked at his watch and at the sun dipping in the sky before getting up and moving to the drive. Squatting down, he turned on the long range radio with wires leading from its open casing to disappear under the drive. Placing the radio into the long grass out of sight, Danny turned, hooked the rifle over his shoulder and started jogging back towards the house. After a quick visit to the barn, Danny entered the kitchen, his face, jeans and jacket smeared black with axle grease, making Nicki and Scott jump. He placed two long range radios and the rifle on the table and dumped the pillowcase, knotted at the open end on a chair.

'Don't touch that, Scotty boy,' Danny said, spotting Scott out of the corner of his eye moving curiously towards it, as he pulled a couple of knives from the kitchen block and put them in his jacket pocket.

'Do you mind sharing, dear boy? Enquiring minds would like to know what's going on,' said Scott, already guessing that the shit was about to hit the fan.

'Blazer's men, two cars, eight-man hit team. Best guess, they're waiting until it's dark. It's what I'd do.'

'So what do we do?' said Nicki, the fear visible on her face.

'You and Scott pack up your stuff. Now, when I say, go upstairs and lock yourselves in the bathroom. Don't come out until I return,' Danny said, his face hard as granite and eyes dark and menacing.

'But there's eight of them,' Nicki said, tears forming in her eyes.

'Don't worry, I'll be ok,' said Danny, his face softening by her concern.

'Trust Daniel, my dear, this is what he does. The best thing we can do is keep out the way and let him get on with it,' said Scott, packing his laptop up.

Giving in, Nicki did as Danny said and packed up her stuff. Danny stripped and checked the hunting rifle before counting out the six bullets he had for it. When he'd done, he turned off the kitchen light and sat in the dark, staring out the window, motionless. At three minutes past eight, one of the radios sounded.

Click, click, click, click.

'Take this and go upstairs now. Anyone other than me comes in, shoot them,' Danny said, already up out of his seat.

He handed the rifle and bullets to Scott, then picked up the radios and put them in his jacket pocket already heading outside as Scott and Nicki rushed up the stairs to the bathroom.

CHAPTER 28

The cars drove slowly up the dirt drive with their lights off. They drove over the dirt covered metal panel Danny had buried earlier. The car's weight caused it to flex downwards causing the pair of bare ended wires to touch and make contact. The other ends were soldered onto the call button of the radio hidden in the grass, sending out a click every time a tyre went over it.

They continued a little further, stopping three hundred metres short of the farmhouse before exiting the vehicles. All dressed in black with tactical vests and sidearms, the men opened the boot of the cars and loaded up with silenced MP5 submachine guns and magazines.

'Ok, you four go wide and approach the far side of the house. Karl and Atama, you take the right. Me and Jedda will take centre. No heroics, no questioning them. The boss just wants them taken care of, so just kill them, right. We'll put the bodies on the trailer by the barn, drive them out across the grazing land, and bury them where no one will ever find them. Everyone got it?' said Maaka, hearing the multiple grunts of agreement from the men. 'Ok, let's go.'

The men split and moved off as clouds moving in over the mountains covered the moons glow, taking the visibility down to a few metres and leaving the farmhouse just visible as a silhouette against the horizon. The four men went wide, then split into two pairs, completing a large horseshoe shape with Karl and Atama, and Maaka and Jedda before they turned in and slowly closed in on the farmhouse.

'Hey, Haskin, what's that?'

'What's what?' whispered Haskin to Keats by his side.

'Listen.'

He stood still.

Click, click.

'I don't know, it's coming from over there by the tree,' said Haskin, moving forward cautiously.

Click, click.

They got within a few metres of the sound as the clouds blew past. The moon's light shone through a hole in the clouds, allowing them to see the long range radio leaning against the base of a tree. If they'd looked behind them, they would have seen the whites of Danny's eyes as they flicked open, his body emerging from its covering of dirt and long grass. Dropping his radio as he popped into a squat, Danny yanked two ropes buried in the dirt towards him. Ahead of Haskin and Keats, a large section of electric fence wire woven into a net whipped out of the dirt and engulfed them, the painful shocks caused by the two large batteries buried near their feet caused them to spasm. Haskin's finger locked on the trigger, setting off a semiautomatic burst of three bullets into Keats, the silencer keeping the noise down to soft metallic pings. Before Keats had hit the ground, Danny was behind Haskin, sliding a kitchen knife into the base of his skull before recoiling, shaking off the pain as the electric fence voltage shot up his arm.

Danny spun around and flattened himself against a tree. Another cloud covered the moon, blending him into its silhouette. He looked around the trunk towards the next two men. It took him a moment to locate them in the darkness, eventually spotting their shadowy outline still heading towards the farmhouse, unaware that two of their colleagues were down. Picking up the radio from the base of the tree, Danny clicked it to channel one and slid it back into his jacket pocket before grabbing one of the dropped MP5s and peeling away silently, melting into the darkness. By the time he'd worked his way behind the next two men and Maaka and Jedda, they were only twenty-five metres from the house. Maaka and Jedda were getting close to a low fence post Danny had knocked in as a marker.

Lying on his front, Danny pulled the radio out of his pocket and held it with his finger tensing on the call button. 'Fire in the hole,' he whispered, clicking the call button down.

At the same time, Maaka eyed the freshly knocked-in fence post and noticed the disturbed section of earth ahead of them.

'Jedda, get back!' he shouted, grabbing Jedda's shoulder as the ground erupted in an earth shattering explosion of flame and screws and metal, all travelling at supersonic speed.

Jedda caught the brunt of the blast, blowing him into Maaka as the two flew twenty feet back, sharp screws and bits of metal shredding Jedda's torso and face, before he landed heavily on top of Maaka, with neither of them moving.

The two men on the far side turned at the explosion, lit

up by the flames and caught out in the open like sitting ducks. Danny took them out with two short bursts of fire, dropping them where they stood. Spinning around on his belly in the dirt, Danny tried to locate Karl and Atama. The ground around him popped with puffs of dirt as bullets buried into it. Rolling to one side, Danny sprang to his feet and ran for the nearest tree, letting off short bursts of fire to keep Karl and Atama's heads down. Another burst came his way before he reached cover, tearing through his jeans and gouging the flesh on the outside of his thigh. A second bullet caught the MP5, ripping it from his grip. Flattening himself against the trunk of the tree, Danny took a second to calm his breathing before running full pelt in a straight line, keeping the tree between him and the line of fire until darkness swallowed him up. Turning, he ignored the burning sensation in his leg and sprinted for the back door to the farmhouse.

'Where the fuck is he?' said Karl, lying on his front looking down his gun sight.

'I think you got him. Wait, there. He's gone around the side of the house,' said Atama, catching a glimpse of Danny before he disappeared behind the house.

'Let's go,' growled Karl, leaping to his feet and running for the front door.

'What about Maaka?' said Atama, running after him.

'Fuck him, he's dead, let's finish this,' said Karl, opening the door and sweeping in, his gun up as he looked down it across the kitchen. Atama moved in behind him.

'You take the stairs, I'll check out the living room and follow you up,' said Karl, stopping at the opening to the living room with the stairs to his left.

Atama nodded and headed up, his movements precise and controlled. He didn't make a sound.

Karl moved just inside the living room. Keeping his rifle in one hand, he slid the other along the wall as he felt for the light switch, his eyes always on the room, searching the darkness for movement. He flicked the switch as soon as he found it. The 500-watt halogen worklight Danny had wired into the ceiling rose blinded him instantly. Flicking it back off, Karl swung his rifle left and right as he tried desperately to blink away the white stars dancing across his eyes.

Rising from the darkest corner of the room, Danny exploded forward, opening the pillowcase and throwing the contents in Karl's face. Making out an object flying towards him through his starry vision, Karl instinctively caught it. By the time his brain processed the cold, scaly skin, the eastern tiger snake had struck twice, biting him on the cheek then deep on the neck. Throwing it to the ground, Karl blew it to pieces with a burst of fire. He stepped back and tried to raise his rifle at Danny, but the neurotoxin from the snakebite was already coursing through his veins, attacking his nervous system. His fumbling fingers dropped the rifle as pain racked his body. He stumbled backward, falling onto the kitchen floor, his body hit by seizures. Picking up Karl's rifle, Danny headed up the stairs, moving with the same precise movement as Atama. He didn't make a sound.

CHAPTER 29

Atama turned his head. He'd just finished searching the second bedroom when he sensed, not heard, someone coming up the stairs. Someone quiet, stealthy, dangerous, and definitely not Karl. He turned and moved along the wall towards the door, feeling every footstep before he put his full weight down to make sure it didn't creak and give his position away. He waited to one side of the doorway, listening, the sound of his own breathing and his heart pounding making it hard to tell if he could hear breathing on the other side of the wall. Counting to three in his head, Atama spun into the doorway. A silhouette moved in identical synchronicity, spinning around in front of him as if he were looking in a mirror. Both men reacted by darting a hand forward, catching the barrel of each other's rifles and pushing them skywards as they pulled the triggers. A stream of metallic pings echoed off the walls as plaster from the bullet-riddled ceiling rained down on them. Expelled bullet casings bounced off the walls before tumbling to the floor.

Both guns emptied in seconds.

COMMAND TO KILL

Danny powered his head forward as the last casing hit the ground, headbutting Atama square on the bridge of his nose, sending him flying back into the bedroom, his empty rifle clattering to the ground. But Atama didn't go down. He snorted the blood from his broken nose and spat it on the floor. Standing ready to attack, Atama drew a six-inch commando knife from his tactical vest. Danny dropped his rifle, reached into his jacket, and pulled out a kitchen knife. He moved inside the room as the clouds outside cleared, the moon's glow pouring in through the windows, lighting them up with silvery outlines. Both men circled each other, looking for an opening, both having to believe one hundred percent that they were better than the other man.

Atama broke first, a silver blur cutting through the air, the blade slicing through the fabric of Danny's jacket as he jumped back. Countering as Atama's blade moved away, Danny stabbed forward, his blade digging into Atama's tactical vest but failing to cut through the kevlar lining. Atama came back with lightning speed, his knife sparking as Danny shot the kitchen knife into its path, locking blades with a grating metallic scrape. They both held the tension, muscle pushing against muscle as their predatory eyes stayed locked in the moonlit room. Atama swung a knee into Danny's side. Danny tensed to keep from crumpling, and powered a fist into Atama's already broken nose, sending him staggering back, fighting the watery tears filling his eyes.

Outside, the clouds floated back across the moon, sucking the light out of the room until both men were barely visible. Without taking his eyes off Atama, Danny stepped back away from the window, his outline swallowed in the inky black space at the back of the room. Still staring in Danny's direction with the commando knife raised, Atama pinched the bridge of his broken nose with his other hand, crunching it until it clicked back into place before blowing the blood out of his nostrils. Letting his eyes and brain accustom to the darker room, Atama could just make out the black on black outline of Danny's jacket. Going from still to killing motion in a split second, he exploded forward, thumping the commando knife deep into fabric until it dug into a hard surface. Before Atama's brain could register the empty jacket hung on the wardrobe door, Danny was behind him, the kitchen knife pulling across Atama's neck, slicing deep as it severed his windpipe and cut his carotid artery.

'You ain't that fucking good,' Danny whispered in his ear before backing away.

Atama fell to his knees, his blood pressure dropping like a stone, a gurgling sound coming from his throat as blood ran down his windpipe. He was unconscious within seconds and dead by the time he thumped onto the floor. Danny pulled Atama's commando knife out of the wardrobe and walked out of the room. Heading down the hall, he stood to one side of the bathroom door.

'Oi, Scott, don't blow my bollocks off, it's me,' he said, reaching across and tapping lightly on the door.

The lock slid back, and the door opened a crack to reveal Scott's wide eyes and the barrel of the hunting rifle.

'You took your time, old man. Nicki's been going out of her mind. She's—' said Scott, falling silent when Danny flicked on the hall light, exposing his blood splattered t-shirt.

'Don't worry, it's not mine. I think now might be a good time to get the fuck out of here,' Danny said, seeing Nicki's red, tearful eyes look round from behind Scott.

'Yes, quite. It might be a good idea to change first,' Scott said, opening the door fully.

Still shaking, Nicki moved past him and threw her arms around Danny, sobbing uncontrollably.

'Hey, it's alright, I'm ok,' Danny said, feeling awkward for a few seconds before giving in and putting his arms around her.

'Er, sis, I really think we should be going,' Scott eventually said.

She pulled away, took a deep breath and nodded before the three of them headed down stairs.

'Not that way, go out the back door,' Danny said, guiding them into the living room while trying to fill the doorway to the kitchen and Karl, still convulsing on the floor as the snake's neurotoxin moved further around his body. 'Go and get in the car. It's around the back of the barn. I've just got to wash this blood off and get a new top. I'll be there in a minute.'

Scott and Nicki did as he said. When they'd gone, Danny stepped over Karl and turned the light on. He stripped off his t-shirt, threw it to one side and washed the blood off his hands and face in the sink. He checked the bullet gouge across his leg. The blood had congealed and formed a scab, so he left it alone. Turning, he headed for his kit bag, noticing Karl's eyes following him hatefully around the room. Danny pulled another top on, threw his kitbag over his shoulder, and headed towards the door. He bobbed down on his haunches beside Karl on the way out. 'See ya pal,' he said, giving him two light slaps on the cheek before walking away, flicking the light off on his way out.

CHAPTER 30

Maaka came round with a jolt. He took a huge intake of breath as his eyes shot open. Pain, confusion and a ringing in his ears overloaded his brain until memory and reasoning re-ordered and replayed the assault and explosion that had knocked him out. Somewhere behind him, he could hear a vehicle driving off down the dirt track at speed. A weight pinned him down as he tried to get up, which he eventually realised was Jedda laying on top of him. Maaka rolled him off and knelt down beside him, rolling him back to check his vitals. He didn't need to. Jedda's face and body were ripped to shreds, with a large part of his forehead missing to expose his brain. Leaving him, Maaka stood up. He could just see the outline of two of his crew to his left, not moving. He knew they were dead, turning away, he heading for the house. Staggering a little, he pushed through the door into the kitchen. Flicking the light on, he saw the bullet-ridden snake before spotting Karl's shaking body lying on the floor.

'Karl, stay with me. Karl.'

Maaka dropped to his knees and slapped Karl's cheeks. His eyes opened and pupils shrank as he focused on Maaka's face.

'Good, hang in there.' Maaka looked at his watch. He'd been out for around fifteen minutes.

Muswellbrook was only about half an hour away. It had a hospital.

Standing up, Maaka headed up the stairs to check if Atama was still alive. It didn't take him long to find his body slumped on the floor in a pool of his own blood.

'Fuck,' Maaka shouted, punching a hole in the bedroom door as he hurried back downstairs.

Moving at speed, Maaka leapt over Karl and headed out the door. He sprinted the three hundred metres to the cars, got in, and tore up the dirt road towards the farmhouse. Within minutes, he'd dragged Karl out and laid him on the back seat. Sweating and breathing heavily, Maaka spun the car around, spraying the side of the farmhouse with gravel before speeding down the dirt track towards the road.

'Control, it's Maaka.'

'Go ahead, Maaka,' said Kyle, frowning at the urgency in Maaka's voice over the control room speakers.

'Get onto Muswellbrook hospital. Tell them I'm bringing a man in with a snake bite, a tiger snake bite. Tell them to have antivenom ready. I'll be there in half an hour.' Maaka said, sliding the car sideways onto the tarmac before flooring the accelerator.

'What about Pearson and the Millers?'

'Gone. Pearson took out the entire team. There's only me and Karl left. Now call the fucking hospital,' Maaka shouted, hanging up and throwing the phone on the seat beside him.

'Call the hospital,' Kyle said to Phil before turning and walking to the rear of the room to make a private call.

'Ah, Kyle, I assume it's done,' came Theo's cheery answer.

'No, Pearson took out Maaka's men. Karl is the only one left, and he's been bitten by a snake. Maaka's taking him to hospital.'

'Pearson, every time it's bloody Pearson. You realise this puts me in a rather awkward position. I've got General bloody Simmonds demanding updates on what's apparently his project now.'

'I told you it was a bad idea dealing with him.'

'Now is not the time for I told you so's, Kyle; now is the time for solutions. Do we know where Pearson and the Millers are?'

'No, we've got Hercules searching for the Audi A8 on ANPR and traffic cams, but nothing as yet. They've probably gone more remote and found somewhere else to hole up.'

'Well, that doesn't help me with the General, does it? As soon as Maaka's out of the hospital with Karl, I want them back here. Oh, before that, get him to do a clean-up at that farmhouse.'

'Already on it, and on the subject of the General, just lie to the man, tell him you've taken care of it.'

'Mmm, lie to the man, that's actually not a bad idea. Let me know when you've found them, Kyle,' Theo said, hanging up.

Kyle walked to the front of the room and looked at a large screen as it scrolled through multiple camera feeds per second, searching for the MacIntyre Group's loaned Audi A8.

Where the hell are you?

CHAPTER 31

'Would you mind enlightening us on what we are doing driving around this housing estate in the middle of the night, Daniel,' said Scott, looking wearily out the window while Danny drove slowly past Muswellbrook's sleeping residents.

'Somehow Blazer tracked us all the way out here. I don't want him to track us all the way back. So I'm after... bingo.' Danny stopped fifty metres short of a black Audi A8. 'Sit tight. I'll be back in a sec.'

Stepping out, Danny looked up and down the street. There was no one about. It was gone ten and all the curtains and blinds were shut. Moving towards the car in a fast walk, Danny pulled Atama's commando knife out as he went. He bobbed down at the front of the car and unscrewed the licence plate with the tip of the knife. As soon as it was free, he moved to the back and did the same with the rear plate. After a quick look around, he was back climbing into the car.

'Here, hold these. We'll swap them down the road. No

one will notice until morning and we'll have changed vehicles by then,' he said, starting the car.

'Top idea, old man,' said Scott, taking the plates.

'But where are we going?' said Nicki from the back.

'How much cash have you got?' said Danny, ignoring the question as he drove down the road.

'Er, let me see, $120.'

'I've got $70,' said Nicki, holding up two notes.

'I've got $60. That's $250. That should be more than enough to get a couple of hotel rooms back in Sydney, maybe out by the airport. I need sleep and time to think.'

'My dear fellow, I'll put it on my card. I don't mind,' said Scott with a smile.

'We can't risk it, Scotty boy, I'm pretty sure they can access your transactions to track us,' Danny said, pulling over again.

He took the plates off Scott and went outside to change them. Hopping back in, Danny drove back through the housing estate to join the main road and head back towards Sydney, secure in the knowledge that Blazer's Hercules computer wouldn't flag them through any traffic cameras.

Just before one in the morning, they rolled into the car park at the Holiday Inn on the outskirts of the airport. Danny parked over on the farthest side of the car park, making sure the cameras on the hotel couldn't get a clear view of the Audi's number plates. After the long drive, all the adrenaline that flowed through Danny's veins while taking out Maaka's men had long gone. He stepped out with the others, walking into the hotel dead on his feet. He felt a hand slide into his and looked over at Nicki in surprise. She smiled back, a warm smile, an inviting smile he found hard to pull away from.

'Good evening, how may I help you?' said the night staff on the desk.

'How much for two rooms with late checkout,' Danny said, yawning.

'That will be $100 each room, with a twelve o'clock checkout.'

'Perfect, we'll take them.'

'Names please.'

Danny was about to speak when Nicki stepped forward. 'Mr and Mrs Martin, and one for my brother, Mr Smith,' she said.

The night guy tapped away on his computer. It was late, and he was bored, so he paid no attention to Danny, Nicki, and Scott. 'That will be $200 please,' he said, picking up the card machine.

'That's ok, it'll be cash. We fly home tomorrow and have some left over,' Danny said, managing a smile as he handed over the cash.

'Certainly, sir.' The guy took the money and printed out their receipts before passing them the door keys. 'You're on the third floor, 312 and 320.'

Scott called the lift. Danny looked at the doors and then at the stairs. For once, he gave in and stepped into the lift with Nicki and Scott. They exited out on the third floor. Scott went ahead, slotting the key into 312, opening the door when the lock buzzed.

'Here you are, sis, Daniel and I will be just down the hall.'

To his surprise, Nicki took Danny's hand and pulled him through the door. 'Good night, Scott,' she said.

'I say, do you two really think that's a good idea?' Scott protested.

'Good night, Scott,' came Danny and Nicki's response just before the door closed behind them.

'Right, well, at least I won't have to put up with your smelly feet and snoring,' Scott muttered to himself as he headed down the corridor to his room.

CHAPTER 32

'Listen, Nicki, perhaps Scott's right, perhaps this isn't such a good idea,' Danny said, sitting on the edge of the bed.

'Yeah perhaps he is, this is probably a terrible idea.' Nicki moved up to Danny, cradled his head in her hands, moving her lips to his, kissing him lightly at first and more passionately as he responded.

'I need a shower,' Danny said when they parted.

Nicki looked at him with the remnants of his grease camouflage around his ears and smeared on his jeans. 'Yes, you do.'

Danny stood. He peeled off his top, a blackish-blue bruise showed on his side where Atama had kneed him.

'It's not as bad as it looks.' Danny undid his jeans and eased them down slowly, peeling the material off the congealed blood, careful not to pull the scab off where the bullet had grazed his leg.

'And that, is that as bad as it looks?' Nicki said, taking her top off and sliding out of her jeans.

'It's feeling better by the minute,' Danny said, taking her hand and leading her to the bathroom.

Danny awoke with a start. Light poured in through the gap in the curtains. He turned over to see an empty bed. He sat up fast, ignoring his aching body as the anxiety grew.

'Nicki.'

Relief washed over him when Nicki's smiling face popped out of the bathroom door, a toothbrush in her hand.

'Morning, sleepyhead.'

'Morning, what time is it?'

'Just gone half nine,' she said, losing the toothbrush and walking back into the bedroom, sitting on the bed in her bra and knickers. 'Are you hungry?'

'Starving,' he said, leaning in and kissing her. He slid his arms around her waist and pulled her over him onto her back on the bed.

An hour later they gave Scott a knock. He'd been busy on his laptop, finishing the drone code to upload to Hercules.

'About time too. I've been waiting for you two to, er, surface for ages,' Scott said, closing the laptop and following them along the corridor.

Rested and refreshed, Danny walked past the lift and headed down the stairs to the dining room. Fishing out what little cash they had left, Danny paid for three all-you-can-eat breakfasts.

'So, Daniel, what's the plan?' said Scott at the table.

'First, I'm going to attack the sausages, then I'm going for bacon, eggs and toast,' Danny said, grinning as he stood up.

'Ha ha, yes, very amusing. One would have hoped you were taking our precarious situation seriously.'

'First, one is having breakfast. Once one is stuffed, one will take things seriously, ok, Scotty boy?' Danny said over his shoulder, heading for the breakfast buffet.

'Mmm, and what about you, Nicki? Are you sure you and Daniel are a good idea in the current circumstances?'

'I don't know. I seem to have made the wrong choices ever since I set foot in Oz. Perhaps Danny is the choice I've been looking for all this time,' she replied, her eyes following Danny as he loaded his plate high, before turning to give Scott a smile.

'Alright, my dear, I hope it works out for you both.' Scott reached across the table and took his sister's hand, giving it a squeeze.

'Thanks. Let's get some food.'

The three of them ate well, Danny eventually bottoming out after his third plateful.

'Ok, now it's serious time. You two sit tight. I've got to make some calls before we check out,' Danny said, getting up and heading out.

He fetched the sat phone from the room and went outside to the far side of the car park and waited for satellite lock before making a call.

'Mr Pearson, how good of you to call,' came Simon's smooth Oxford educated voice, answering on the first ring.

'Don't you ever sleep?' Danny said, working out it was nearly 1 am back in London.

'Not recently.'

'Any developments?'

'Yes, some good and some bad. The authorities have

put your little jaunt across Sydney down as some kind of unexplained mass hysteria event. Miss Miller and an unknown white male, that's you, are wanted for questioning due to Miss Miller's vehicle being involved. The good news is all CCTV and camera footage for several blocks around the incident has mysteriously been wiped, thanks to our friend, Mr Blazer. So apart from the motorcycle policeman's description of you and Miss Miller, there's no proof to show that you and Miss Miller were involved.'

'Great, and the good news,' Danny said sarcastically.

'That was the good news, the bad news is General Arthur Simmonds and a Delta Force team just flew into Sydney to put a cork in Blazer's leak, the cork being yourselves.'

'And who the fuck is General Arthur Simmonds?'

'General Simmonds is in charge of Department 23, a little experimental war research facility with a little too much power. They also happen to be the department Blazer sold his project to.'

'Christ, anything else?'

'In the unlikely event you actually live long enough to get me the drone program, my contact in the Australian government can make the police investigation go away, so you will at least be free to fly home and not rot in an Australian jail.'

'Can't your contact just get the Australian Intelligence Services to shut Blazer down?'

'On what grounds? There's no evidence this project exists, no link from the events in the city centre to Blazer; as it stands they would struggle to give the man a parking ticket let alone a full investigation.'

'What if I don't do it? What if we just get a flight home and forget about it?'

'Entirely your choice, dear boy, Mr Blazer may or may not forget all about you. General Simmonds, on the other hand, would not. I have no doubt that someone like yourself can look after themselves, but if the project remains operational, it wouldn't be very hard for the General to orchestrate a little accident to happen to Mr Miller or perhaps his sister.'

'Ok, ok, I'll do it, but I need a few things,' Danny said after a tense pause.

'Tremendous, tell me what you need and I'll see what I can do.'

'To start with, I need transport and a safe place to stay.'

'I'm sure that can be arranged. Anything else?'

'Yes.'

CHAPTER 33

'Will he do it?'

'He will, you just need to know which buttons to press,' said Simon, sipping his drink on the upper deck of the millionaire's yacht, Luna, as it cruised Sydney harbour.

'And which buttons might they be?'

'Mr Pearson has one major flaw: he will predictably choose to protect the innocent at all costs.'

'A noble trait indeed, but not one I imagine you want in an asset. And once you get the program?'

'I will make sure you have the necessary proof of its existence. A little word with the defence committee and the cabinet, and you can finish Theodore Blazer and out the Prime Minister for their financial ties. Add a little rumour-mongering and play your cards right, Malcolm, you could be PM within a month,' Simon said, raising his glass to Malcolm.

'And the American?'

'Ah, the Pentagon man, Joel Stilwell. He's been looking for an excuse to close Department 23 for some time, let's hope the ammunition Agent Johnson has given him, and General Simmonds' unsanctioned deployment of a Delta Force unit on Australian soil, will be enough for him to succeed.'

'And what are you going to do with the drone program?'

'We'll tuck it away in some dark corner with all the other deeply disturbing inventions of man. You have to appreciate the value of it though. Imagine a terrorist leader with a son who has a love of gaming, one little command and said leader is lying dead on the ground with a surprised look on his face, while his son stands over him with a kitchen knife in hand,' said Simon with a smile.

'What happens now?'

'We give Pearson what he asked for and let him do what he does best.'

'And if he fails?' said Malcolm, glancing over at the Opera House as they cruised under Sydney Harbour Bridge.

'Then you'll still be shuffling papers for the PM and I'll be back in London while Mr Blazer will still be operating a global network of unwilling assassins. I guess we'd better hope he doesn't fail, old boy.'

Danny counted out the last of the cash on the hotel bar and ordered three beers. They'd checked out of the rooms an hour ago and were waiting for Simon to come good on Danny's requests.

'How long do you think it'll take?'

COMMAND TO KILL

'Don't know, Scotty boy, we've just gotta be patient, he'll deliver.'

Sitting purposely with a view out of the bar, through the hotel to the entrance door, Danny tensed slightly at the sight of a guy heading in from the car park. His body language and alert eyes rang alarm bells, the man was definitely military trained. He walked in their direction, seeing them without looking straight at them. Danny tensed his legs, sliding slightly to one side on his chair, ready to move. His hand gripped tightly on the beer glass, ready to launch beer in the man's eyes before smashing the glass on the table and stab him in the neck. The tension stayed locked in time, Scott and Nicki totally unaware as Danny watched the man in his peripheral vision get closer. When he got within a few feet, Danny saw the man's hand twitch. He was about to explode into action when he saw a car key drop to the ground. The guy stopped and stooped down. He picked up the key and placed it on the table.

'You dropped your key, mate,' he said, looking Danny straight in the eye before giving him an almost undetectable nod and heading to the bar, where he ordered a beer.

'Drink up, guys, time to go,' Danny said, exhaling, the tension in his body draining away.

The three of them finished up and went out into the car park. Danny pressed the unlock button on the car key until the lights on an unremarkable grey Nissan Qashqai flashed back at him.

'Get in,' he said, walking around the back and opening the boot. Danny put his old kitbag in beside a large, black canvas bag and two sets of registration plates. He unzipped the bag and eyed the contents before zipping it back up again and shutting the boot.

When he climbed in the driver's seat and turned the

STEPHEN TAYLOR

ignition on, the sat nav lit up on the screen in the centre console. Someone had already programmed a destination, the arrow telling Danny to turn right out of the car park.

'I guess we go that way.'

'What was in the boot?' Nicki said looking across at him, the trauma from the last few days showing in her face.

'Just some stuff to even the odds.' Danny smiled at her reassuringly.

CHAPTER 34

'Mr Sunia, you should really stay here for another day or so. There's still venom in your system. You could suffer a relapse.'

Karl ignored the doctor. He pulled the IV needle out of the back of his hand and got out of bed.

'Where are my fucking clothes?' he growled, putting his hand on the bed to steady himself as he stumbled standing up.

'You're not well, Mr Sunia.'

'Bollocks.' Karl yelled, finding his clothes in the bedside cabinet and pulled his jeans on. 'Maaka, Maaka.'

'Yeah, I'm here,' Maaka shouted back from the corridor.

'Get me the fuck out of here!'

Karl pulled his top on and stamped his feet into his boots. He put his arm around Maaka for support and the two headed out of the ward while the doctor shook his head behind them.

'How are you feeling?' said Maaka after he'd helped Karl into the car and driven out of the hospital.

'Like shit, my fucking nerves are jangling like someone electrocuted me. I'm going to get that bastard Pearson and hurt him bad, really fucking bad,' Karl said, his hands and legs shaking while beads of sweat formed on his forehead.

'We've got something to do first,' Maaka said, turning back towards McCullys Gap.

An hour later they were at the farmhouse. They spent some time collecting all the discarded weapons and picking up as many empty bullet casings as they could find, putting them in the car before turning back towards the dead bodies. Karl gulped down water and rested, fighting against the shakes before he helped Maaka drag the dead bodies into the crater caused by Danny's homemade bomb. After another rest, Karl picked up a shovel and helped Maaka shovel dirt until only a level patch of freshly dug dirt remained. Heading off towards the barn, Maaka returned a few minutes later with a large jerry can of petrol. While Karl sat on the bonnet of the car, Maaka went upstairs, pouring petrol throughout the rooms before working his way downstairs. He continued the same process downstairs, kicking the dead snake out of the way as he left out of the kitchen door. Chucking the empty can into the kitchen, Maaka set light to the corner of a cleaning cloth and threw it in through the kitchen door, the fumes of the evaporating petrol catching the fire before the cloth hit the floor. A whoosh of flame ripped through the building and up the stairs in seconds. With smoke and flames rising behind him Maaka walked calmly to the car.

'You ok to drive the other car back?' Maaka said, pointing to the Toyota Land Cruiser parked three hundred metres down the dirt drive.

'Yeah, I'll be alright,' Karl replied.

Maaka spun the car around and dropped Karl at the

other vehicle. The farmhouse roof collapsed in on itself behind them as Karl followed Maaka along the dirt track and onto the main road, accelerating away towards Sydney.

CHAPTER 35

'Maaka and Karl are on their way back now, boss.'

'Thank you, Jeff, any news on our fugitives?' Theo said.

'Nothing on the Audi, nothing on facial and no phone or card transactions,' said Phil, tapping furiously away at his console.

'Ok, keep on it. They'll have to surface sooner or later,' said Theo, turning at the phone ringing on the desk beside him. 'Yes?'

'Mr Blazer, I have a General Simmonds and a number of, er, gentlemen here to see you.'

Shit, what the hell is Simmonds doing here?

'I'm not here, ok? Tell him Mr Drago is on his way down,' Theo said, clicking his fingers at Kyle to get his attention.

'He's very insistent, Mr Blazer, I think he knows your h—'

There was a scuffling sound and bang as the phone dropped, then silence.

'Andrews, hello, Andrews?' said Theo, raising his voice.

'Get your sorry arse down here now, Blazer, trust me, you do not want to make me come up there and get you,' came the General's voice, ordering, not asking.

'General, how wonderful to have you back. I'll be down straight away.' Theo put the phone down fast without waiting for an answer.

'What's up?' said Kyle.

'The General's here. He's down-bloody-stairs. He knows about Pearson and the Millers. I can tell he knows,' Theo said quietly to Kyle, the nerves showing on his face.

'He can't know. There's no way he can know. Just tell him Maaka and his men took care of it,' Kyle said, keeping calm.

'Right, yes, right. You brief this lot while I go down and deal with him, and phone Maaka, tell him not to come here, er, tell him to go to Blazer Games. I'll talk to him later. Anyone asks, Pearson and the Millers are dead.'

Theo left the command room, taking a minute to compose himself and fix a corporate smile on his face ready to tackle the General. He headed down the corridor, fighting rising panic as he looked down from the first floor landing at the General, Agent Johnson and two of the serious-looking Delta team looking up at him from the foyer. The other two Delta team men had Andrews and the other security guard pinned against the wall behind the reception desk.

'General, a pleasure to see you. Gentlemen, would you mind releasing my staff? That's quite unnecessary.'

'Let's go to the command room for a chat,' said the General, walking up the stairs past Theo, ignoring his outstretched hand.

'Of course. If these other gentlemen would like to wait in the canteen while we conduct our business.' said Theo, turning on the stairs and hurrying back up as the whole entourage walked past him. 'General, I must insist, they don't have clearance to enter the command room.'

'Just open the door, Blazer,' the General said, tapping the palm reader next to the reinforced steel door.

With his brain failing to come up with a way to get on top of the situation, Theo placed his palm on the reader and led them through the double set of security doors into the command centre.

'Would you mind telling me what this is all about, General?' Theo said, trying to look as in control as he could.

'You fucked up, Blazer. You think your little stunt in Sydney went unnoticed? It didn't. The deployment of so many drones will alert the Russians. They are bound to investigate the death of their agent, and what was it all for? The goddamn targets got away. You'd better tell me they're taken care of, Blazer.'

'Of course, and let me remind you, General, you were happy for me to run our little demonstration on Natasha Shayk when you were last here. I—'

'That was before you sent multiple drones on the rampage across Sydney. One was a mother and her baby, for Christ's sake.'

'Yes, perhaps I went a little far, but we took care of it, data, cell phones, all CCTV gone. The authorities haven't got a clue what happened,' Theo said, standing tall, his confidence growing as he spoke.

'That remains to be seen, and for the duration of my visit, my men will remain here to oversee the operation. Moving on to other business, I have a small window of opportunity to terminate a high level target. Intel tells me he will be at a particular location at 2 p.m. local time. That's 10 p.m. tonight here,' said the General as the members of the Delta team fanned out and stood at the back of the room, their body language and unwavering stares telling Theo's staff they were not to be messed with.

'Not a problem, General. If you would like to tell my staff the details, we will get a list of drones in the vicinity.'

'Agent Johnson has all the details. I have business to attend to, but I'll be back tonight to oversee the mission,' the General said, turning to leave.

'Of course, General.'

'And Blazer,' he said, turning back.

'Yes.'

'Don't fuck this up.'

CHAPTER 36

The sat nav took them into Woolloomooloo, a suburb just outside of Sydney's bustling centre. They arrived outside a row of three-storey houses tucked a couple of streets back from Hyde Park and the road Danny and Nicki had charged along a few days earlier.

'What do we do now?' said Scott, looking around blankly.

'I don't know. Check the glove box, Scott.'

While Scott did that, Danny flipped down the sun visor, catching a set of house keys as they fell from behind it. He turned them over in his hand, looking at the No 91 written on the paper label tied to the bunch of keys, then over at number 91 beside them.

'Are we just going to sit here all day or are we going in?' Nicki said, already opening the door to get out.

Danny looked at Scott and shrugged, opening the door to get out next to Nicki. He moved to the boot and opened it, unzipping the bag far enough to grab a Glock 17 handgun out. Tucking it in the back of his jeans under his jacket, Danny grabbed the canvas bag and his old kit bag and hooked them on his shoulder. He walked up the steps to the front door, trying to disguise how heavy the bag was as he went. As soon as he'd opened the door, Danny dropped the bags on the floor, grabbing the Glock from his jeans. He moved ahead of Scott and Nicki, sweeping each room as he went. Scott shook his head and headed for the kitchen as Danny disappeared upstairs.

'Would you care for a coffee, sis?' he said, clicking the kettle on before sniffing the milk from the fridge.

'Yes please,' she said, following him into the kitchen.

'Do ask our resident caveman if he would like one, when he's done whatever it is he's doing.'

'It's all clear. You can relax,' Danny said, reappearing.

'How reassuring, old boy. Tea? Coffee?' Scott said, shaking a mug at him.

'Er, coffee. You can't be too careful, Scotty boy.'

'Well, I feel safer anyway,' Nicki said, leaning in to give Danny a kiss on the cheek.

'And it's appreciated, Daniel. Now, how are we going to get Blazer's palm print data from Blazer Games?'

Danny smiled and headed for the front door. Picking up the heavy canvas bag, he brought it through and put it down on the kitchen table. Unzipping it, he emptied the contents, placing it neatly across the table.

'Hmm, I get the cash, guns, the burner phones and those little explosive looking things. Very you. But what's with the Douglas Pratt Plumbers outfit?' said Scott, sliding a shoulder holster aside to put the coffee cups down.

'I'll show you,' said Danny, opening one of the pay as you go phone boxes. 'Google me the number for Blink Defence Systems, can you, Scott?'

Scott opened his laptop bag and did as Danny asked,

spinning the laptop around so he could see the number as he started dialling.

'Hi, this is Tim on security over at Blazer Games. Is Mr Blazer there?'

'Mr Blazer is in a meeting and not to be disturbed. Can I take a message?' said the receptionist.

'Yes, can you tell him there is a problem, the reception toilet's backing up. I've called the plumbers. They will be here in a couple of hours, but I'm finishing my shift now. Please could you ask Mr Blazer to clear Douglas Pratt Plumbers and put them on the visitors' schedule for the night staff?'

'Thank you, Tim, I'll make sure Mr Blazer gets the message.'

Hanging up, Danny put the phone down and took a big gulp of coffee. 'Right, this is the plan. Blazer's not at home, he's in a meeting at Blink, so we go to his apartment, break in, and leave you there waiting for the palm access code, so you can copy the drone program and change the command code. I'll go to Blazer Games dressed as the expected plumber and you can talk me through the security computer thing, and away we go.'

'And what do I do?' said Nicki.

'You stay here until we return.'

'I don't want to stay here. I want to help.'

'No, it's too dangerous. I need you to stay here where it's safe,' Danny said, not wanting to be argued with.

'I'm afraid that's not going to work, old boy. As much as I'd like my sister to stay here, the thought of talking you and your sausage fingers through the technical aspects of cracking and extracting information out of a secure computer system does not fill me with confidence.'

'You could talk me through it.'

'With all due respect, Daniel, you're a caveman. It'll

take me over an hour to get you to turn on the laptop, let alone access their computer, find the encrypted data file and email it to me,' said Scott sipping his coffee.

The room went silent. Danny sat back in a kitchen chair looking from Nicki, who was obviously annoyed with him, to Scott, who he knew was right.

'Ok, you're coming, but you do exactly as I say, ok, and we've got to do something about your hair,' he eventually said, finding it hard to stay serious when Nicki's face lit up.

CHAPTER 37

Driving the grey Nissan Qashqai to the speed limit, Danny took a detour on the way to Theodore Blazer's home, pulling in at a DIY store. He left Scott and Nicki in the car, returning fifteen minutes later with a tool belt, a tough canvas tool bag and a selection of hand tools.

'Oh look, it's Super Mario,' said Scott out the window.

'Great, does that make me Luigi?' Nicki said, pulling her freshly dyed brown hair up in a ponytail.

'I'm afraid it does, my dear. You'd look good with a moustache.'

'Shut up, idiot.'

Danny opened the boot and put the tools in, leaving it open as he walked over to the grass and dirt strip beside the car park.

'What are you doing?' Nicki shouted out the window.

'We can't turn up looking like it's our first day on the job,' Danny replied, throwing the canvas tool bag and tool belt in the dirt before jumping up and down on them and kicking them around. He returned to the car, ignoring the strange looks from other shoppers as they came and went.

'Wow, he's really taking this disguise thing seriously.'

'Quite. I think he might actually fix their plumbing,' chuckled Scott.

Chucking the bag and belt in the boot, Danny shut it and got back in the driver's seat, looking quizzically at Scott and Nicki laughing. 'What?'

'Nothing, my good man, drive on,' Scott said with a smile.

A short drive later they drove alongside Sydney's famous Bondi Beach. The sun was starting to dip in the sky and the last of the day's surfers were loading their boards onto the roof racks of various cars and stereotypical VW Camper vans.

'Where's Blazer's place?'

'Just down there at the south end of the beach. See that big block of apartments above the cliff?' Nicki said, leaning forward and pointing it out between the front seats. 'The whole top floor is his.'

Danny pulled into the car park, finding a space in between a Maserati and a top of the range Land Rover. He turned to look over his shoulder at the entrance with its door entry system to one side.

'How are we going to get in?' said Nicki, following his gaze.

'Get your stuff ready, Scott, and stand beside that Mercedes like you just got out of it.'

'Ok, what are you going to do?' said Scott, eyeing the car Danny was talking about.

'I'm going to get someone to let us in. Follow my lead, ok?'

'Er, ok, now?'

'Yes, Scott, now,' Danny said, getting out.

He opened the boot and chucked a few tools into the tool bag while Scott and Nicki walked across the car park and stood either side of the Mercedes. Taking the tool bag out, Danny shut the boot and moved around to the driver's side of the Land Rover. He took a quick look around before sliding a crowbar out of the bag and cracking the window with a short sharp jab. The second the window shattered, showering the driver's seat in a million glass crystals, the car alarm wailed. In the same second, Danny had the crowbar back into the bag and was walking across the car park to the entrance door. He immediately pressed the buzzer for the first apartment, moving on to the next button when no one answered after fifteen seconds. On the third try, a man's voice answered.

'Hello?'

'Hi, I'm looking for the owner of the Land Rover in the car park. Some kids just broke the window and legged it. I don't know if they took anything,' Danny said, emphasising urgency in his voice.

'Er, Land Rover, blue?'

'Yeah.'

'That's Bruce's. He's in apartment twelve.'

'Thanks,' Danny said, pressing the buttons.

'Hello?'

'Hi, is that Bruce?'

'Yes, who's this?'

'The guy in three said the blue Land Rover's yours. Some kids just broke the window and legged it. I don't know if they took anything.'

'Oh, shit, I'm coming. I'll be right down.'

Danny gave a thumbs-up to Scott and Nicki, turning back in time to see Bruce racing down the stairs. He yanked the door open and stepped out. Danny dropped the tool bag on the doorstep as he turned, stopping the door clicking shut.

'Sorry, mate, I saw them as I was pulling up and they just legged it.'

'Well, thanks anyway. Little bastards.'

'Look, I've gotta go. My customer's just turned up and I've got a leaky tap on three to fix. Good luck with the window,' Danny said, waving to Scott, who headed for the entrance door with Nicki.

'No worries, thanks for taking the time to buzz me,' Bruce said, wandering off to his car.

Picking his bag up as he followed Scott and Nicki inside, the three of them headed up the stairs to the penthouse apartment on the top floor.

'Are you going to pick the lock, old boy?'

'In a manner of speaking, Scotty,' Danny said, dropping the bag and sliding the crowbar out again. With unexpected speed, Danny jammed the sharp end in between the door and the wooden frame as hard as he could, jerking the bar back towards himself, popping the door open as the wooden surround splintered away from the lock.

'After you,' Danny said with a grin.

'Why thank you, kind sir,' said Nicki, walking inside.

'Subtle as always, Daniel,' Scott said, rolling his eyes as he stepped over the splintered bits of wood on the floor.

Danny followed the two through the luxury apartment, looking at the view of Bondi Beach through the wall-to-wall glass sliding doors lining the kitchen. He continued down the corridor, turning into Blazer's office to see Scott unzipping his laptop bag as he sat in Theo's Hans J. Wegner seat in front of the six screen computer setup and the palm reader on one side.

'All good, Scott?'

'Yes, just don't take too long getting back here, ok?'

'We'll send you the palm print data and get back here ASAP,' Danny said, reaching inside the tool bag. He pulled out a Glock handgun, clicked the safety off and placed it on the desk. Reaching in the bag again, he pulled out a bag of zip ties, slid out a handful and put them next to the gun. 'Blazer or anyone else comes through that door, point that at them and zip tie them to a chair. Be careful, Scotty boy, the safety's off.'

'Ok, just go, and keep my little sister safe.'

Danny nodded to his best friend and left, with Nicki close behind.

CHAPTER 38

It was dark when they pulled into Blazer Games' near-empty car park. Danny parked to one side, keeping the car out of view from the security desk. They would see it on the CCTV monitors, but the night security staff would barely give it a look on the tiny screen.

'You ready?'

'Yep,' Nicki said with false confidence.

'Ok, remember to stand slightly behind me and keep the peak of your hat tilted down. They won't recognise you.'

'What if they do?'

'They won't, the purple hair's gone and they're not expecting to see you as a plumber's mate. People only see what they want to see, you'll be fine,' Danny said, getting out of the car.

Grabbing the tool belt and bag, Danny headed for the entrance with Nicki close behind. As the doors slid apart, he approached the desk with the smile and confidence of a man who was supposed to be there.

'Evening, guys, Douglas Pratt Plumbers. I've got a call out for a problem with the reception toilets.'

'Ok, if you could just sign the visitors' book for me, I'll just call and find out what's—'

'It's ok, Bill, they're on the visitors' list. Mr Drago authorised it. I'll take them round to the toilets,' said Gregg.

Gregg came round the desk and walked ahead of Danny and Nicki. They followed him down a corridor away from the desk.

'Hey, you don't see many female plumbers around, especially not as good looking as you. Do I know you? You look kinda familiar,' Gregg said, trying to look cool as he looked back over his shoulder.

'Yeah, you won't be saying that when I'm up to my elbows in shit from clearing this toilet out,' Nicki answered abruptly.

Gregg's smile dropped and he faced forward again. Danny looked at her with a grin.

'What?' she mouthed back.

Just before the toilets they passed a locked door. Nicki nodded towards it.

'Right, we're here, men's toilets this side, ladies' the other.'

Hey, buddy, have you got a key for that door?' Danny said, still smiling as he pointed to the one Nicki had nodded to.

'Er, yeah. But there's no plumbing in there,' Gregg said, instinctively looking down at the keychain on his belt.

When he looked up, all he saw was four knuckles heading for his face as Danny planted a blow between the eyes, knocking him through the door into the men's toilet.

'Oi, sexy plumber, shout me if anyone comes, I won't

be a sec,' Danny said, pulling some zip ties out of his tool belt and winking at Nicki before going into the toilets.

He emerged a minute later with the keychain in hand, walked across to the locked door and riffled through the keys until one clicked the lock open. The two of them slid into a small room containing several data cabinets.

'Ok, let's see, phone systems, CCTV unit. Mmm, here we are, door entry system,' Nicki said, opening a cabinet door as she fished her laptop out of Danny's tool bag.

'How do you know that's it?' Danny said, looking at all the blinking lights, network cables, and computers in the cabinets.

'Er, it's written on the door,' Nicki said, moving her head to show the Door Entry System label.

'Oh, right, you crack on. I'll watch the door.'

Nicki plugged in the laptop and called Scott while it booted up.

'About time. It feels like I've been sitting here forever.'

'Not long now, bro. I've booted up the laptop you prepped and plugged it into the door entry system PCs USB drive.'

'Ok, my dear. If you turn the monitor on, the PC should be asking for a password. Use the mouse and click inside the password box.'

'Yep, done that.'

'Now you will see a little icon I've installed on your laptop called Safe Cracker. Double click that for me, sis.'

Nicki did as Scott asked and watched a box appear on the laptop. Letters, numbers and characters scrolled on the laptop and in the PCs password box as the software ripped through the billions of password possibilities.

'How long will it take?'

'Er, let me see, eight-digit password, that's 200 billion

combinations, latest processor, x combinations per minute. Mmm, 22 minutes maximum, likelihood 10 to 15 minutes.'

'And once we're in?' said Nicki, watching the first digit of the combination lock in.

'That's the easy bit. I just need you to find the door entry system file and then find the palm print data folder. Open it and select Theodore Blazer, then copy it to the laptop and email it to me. How's it doing?'

'Third digit has just locked in.'

'Good, not long now.'

Danny opened the door a crack. He looked up and down the empty corridor before easing the door shut again. He was about to try and hurry Nicki up, but could see by the look on her face, she was already stressed out and thought better of it.

Come on, Nicki, this is taking too long.

CHAPTER 39

'You alright, Karl? Jesus, mate, you're sweating like a pig,' Maaka said.

'I'll manage. I'll feel a whole lot better once I kill that bastard Pearson,' said Karl, taking out his handgun and locking his arm forward as if he were about to shoot. His hand still shook from the effects of the snakebite, but with a little extra concentration, Karl managed to get it down to a mild tremor.

'Put that away, we'll be there in a minute,' Maaka ordered, turning at the lights, giving them a view of Blazer Games at the end of the street.

'What are we doing here anyway?' Karl said, sliding the gun back into its shoulder holster before draining a bottle of water.

'Drago said the General's flown in with some muscle. He doesn't trust Blazer after that cluster fuck in the city centre. Blazer still hasn't told him Pearson and the Millers got away and wants us out of sight until the General fucks off back to Uncle Sam.'

STEPHEN TAYLOR

They turned into Blazer Games and parked up in front of the entrance doors.

'Good evening, Mr Carter, Mr, er, Sunia,' Bill said, smiling at Maaka, his face dropping at the sight of Karl's blotchy, sweating face and bandaged neck.

Karl just snarled back at him and turned to Maaka. 'Bloody water's going through me. I'm off for a piss.'

'Sorry, the toilets are out of use, the plumbers are in there,' Bill shouted after him.

'Then they better move or I'll piss on them,' Karl shouted back.

'Are we done?'

'Scott, you got it?'

'Just one minute, sis,' said Scott, a ping sounding in the background. 'That's it. Pack it up and get back here.'

'On our way,' Nicki said, flipping the laptop down and unplugging it from the door entry system PC before sliding it back into Danny's tool bag.

'Let's go.'

'Hang on, someone's coming,' Danny said, easing the crack in the door shut again and placing his ear to the wooden surface.

Turning down the corridor, Karl marched up to the

men's toilet and pushed through the door, expecting to have to tell the plumbers to get out. He was surprised to find the toilets empty. He walked up to the urinal and relieved himself.

'Ah, fuck, that's better.'

He washed his hands then splashed his face to freshen up. He was drying off with the paper towels when he heard a moaning from one of the cubicles. Within a second Karl had dropped the paper towel and pulled the gun from his shoulder holster. He stepped over and pushed the door slowly open with the barrel of the gun, stopping when Gregg's two black eyes looked back at him, wide and scared. They went wider when Karl pulled a flick knife out of his pocket and clicked it open. He slid it under the guard's tie, used as an improvised gag, slicing the ultra-sharp blade through the material.

'Talk.'

'The bloody plumber punched me in the face and tied me up.'

'What did he look like?'

'There were two of them, a big bloke, dark hair, about your size.'

'And the other one?' Karl growled as he popped the zip ties binding the man.

'A woman, good looking. I was sure I'd seen her somewhere before.'

'Pearson and the Miller woman.' Karl backed out of the cubicle, nearly pulling the toilet door off its hinges as he hurried into the corridor. 'Maaka, they're here, Pearson and the Miller woman,' he yelled on his way to reception.

'Shit, covers blown,' Danny said, taking his ear off the door.

'What do we do now?'

'Is there another way out of here?' Danny said, spotting the CCTV system label on the cabinet in front of him.

'There's a loading bay below the R&D department. That's if I can still get in.'

'Let's do it,' Danny said, waving Nicki back as he opened the door to the CCTV system. He pulled the crowbar out and jabbed it through the plastic front of the PC, driving it into the internal components with a flash and a puff of smoke as the unit died. 'At least they won't be able to watch where we go.'

Danny pulled a gun from the tool bag and handed it to Nicki, then pulled out some extra magazines and little explosive devices and put them in his pockets before abandoning the bag. Pulling his own gun out, he opened the door a crack, listening to Karl and Maaka's raised voices from reception. He looked through the crack to see the corridor was clear.

'Which way?'

'Past the toilets to the end of the corridor, there are stairs to the first floor and the entrance to the R&D department.'

'Ok, stay close to me,' he said, looking Nicki straight in the eyes to make sure she was focused. She nodded back at him.

They moved out into the corridor and headed away from reception. When they got level with the men's toilets, the door opened. Danny whipped the gun around, only easing his finger on the trigger at the last moment when Gregg's frightened face registered in his mind. Lowering the gun in his right hand, Danny powered a left hook into the guard's already painful face. For the second time that night, Gregg flew back into the toilets. Danny was already moving towards the stairs to the R&D department before the toilet door swung shut, closely followed by Nicki.

CHAPTER 40

'What the fuck do you mean they're here?'

'The plumbers, it's them, Pearson and the Miller woman. They tied up the security guy. They're somewhere in the building,' said Karl, pushing the other security man out of the way as he ran around the reception desk to the CCTV monitors. 'Fuck, the cameras are down.'

'Should I call Mr Blazer?' said Bill, lifting the phone receiver.

'Put that phone down,' said Maaka, pointing his gun at Bill's head. 'Good, now lock the entrance doors. If they come this way, shoot them.'

'Let's go,' growled Karl, jumping over the desk before heading towards the corridor.

Karl flattened himself against the wall with Maaka automatically falling in behind him, the years of military service alleviating the need for conversation. Karl swung round the corner, his eyes running down the gunsight at the empty corridor, the adrenaline and thrill of the chase calming his shakes.

'Clear,' he said, triggering Maaka to move swiftly down the corridor.

Hitting the wall, Maaka darted his gun into the open door to the security systems room. He spotted the door to the CCTV cabinet open and wisps of smoke rising from the its busted up PC. He was about to move away when he spotted the open cabinet door to the door entry system. A canvas tool bag sat on the floor in front of it with Nicki's laptop protruding from the top.

What the hell were you up to?

'Clear,' he shouted, returning to cover the corridor as Karl moved swiftly past him to take point. The door to the men's toilet opened as he approached it. Gregg emerged, his eyes black, and blood streaming from his nose as he gripped the door frame, just about managing to hold himself upright.

'Get out the fucking way,' Karl snarled.

Turning his hand to the side, Karl lashed out, cracking Gregg in the face with the butt of his handgun, the blow knocking him back into the toilets where he lay on the floor, unconscious.

'Here goes the moment of truth,' Nicki said, pressing her hand on the palm reader next to the R&D door, she breathed a sigh of relief when the electric door lock clicked open.

'I guess luck's on our side. Ladies first.' Danny said, pushing the door open for Nicki.

As she entered the security office with its lockers and metal detector, Danny had a last look up and down the corridor, just in time to see Karl kick the door from the stairwell open to dart a look from one side. Their eyes locked briefly, Karl's face contorting in anger as they levelled their guns and let off simultaneous bursts of fire before rolling away behind cover. Karl's bullets digging into the wall behind Danny, while Danny's punched neat holes through the door to the stairs.

'Spoke too soon, get the other door open, Nicki, we've got incoming.'

Nicki jumped through the metal detector, ignoring its buzz and red light as her gun set it off. She slapped her hand on the palm reader beside the R&D entrance door; it scanned green before turning red with an access denied message written above it.

'It won't open,' she shouted, placing her palm on it again, only to get the same result.

'Shit, hang on.'

Going low, Danny put his gun into the corridor and leant out far enough to get one eye down its sight towards the stairwell. He saw a flash of hair and an eye as Karl darted another look. Firing off another three rounds, Danny tore off chunks of the door frame where Karl's face had been a split second earlier.

That should give me a minute.

'Get behind the lockers,' Danny shouted, shutting the door before jumping through the buzzing metal detector, reaching in his pocket, Danny pulled out two little devices. Peeling off some tape on the back, he slapped them over the hinges of the heavy door. Setting the timers to fifteen seconds, he hit the enter button and slid over the security man's desk, joining Nicki behind the metal lockers as the timers beeped down towards zero.

'I can't see him. I think he's gone into the R&D department.'

'On three, cover me. One, two, three.' Maaka charged past Karl with his gun trained on the R&D door. He headed for the nearest office, twisting the doorknob to open the door and crouch half in and half out of the opening for cover, his gun never leaving the R&D door. 'Clear.'

Karl broke cover, moving past Maaka, his gun up as he slid along the wall towards the R&D door. He got within a few feet when an explosion pounded the wall against his back. The R&D door banged loudly as debris hit the back of it, sending a cloud of dust curling up into the corridor from the gap underneath.

'What the fuck?' Karl yelled, stumbling back, holding his ringing ears.

Moving past him, Maaka got to the door and slammed his palm on the reader beside it. The green light scanned half way down before blinking and going off. The door didn't click open. 'Shit.'

Full of anger and hate, Karl joined him, punching the reader as hard as he could before trying again. The green light scanned all the way down and the door lock clicked. They eased the door open, scanning the trashed room before entering. As the dust cloud cleared, they saw the hole into the R&D department, its bent-up entrance door sitting on its side, wedged in the middle of a broken desk.

CHAPTER 41

'Let's see, just execute that and hit enter, and hey presto.'

The second Scott entered the palm reader code for Theodore Blazer, the six screens burst into life with streams of data and mirror images of the command centre's main screens.

'Oh, you're good, Mr Miller. You're very good,' Scott muttered to himself, a smug smile on his face. 'Now let's have a little look at the program files, shall we?'

He moved through Hercules' vast system, searching folders and program files until he found one called Drone Program. When he delved further, he found all the extended Command to Kill program files for players who passed the game's suggested triggers, and the database of all the primed players who had completed the program, ready to do Blazer's bidding.

'I think it's time to put a spanner in the works.'

Linking his fingers, Scott turned his palms out and extended his arms, cracking his knuckles before attacking the keyboard at a blinding speed. Within a few minutes, he'd hit the copy button and was watching a progress bar creep across the screen as files copied from Hercules to his laptop, ready to give to Simon so he could shut Blazer down. When it completed, Scott uploaded his replacement file to Hercules before firing out his overriding trigger command via text message, email, and game chat to all the people on the database. A good percentage of drones would be uncontrollable straight away. The rest would get his message as the day went on, as they finished work or awoke across the world's different time zones.

'Now, let's just hide my tracks.'

Scott started opening files and altering the entry log to hide his changes before deleting the new command program so nobody but him knew the command to trigger the drones.

'Now, what shall I do while I wait? Hmm, I wonder if I can get access to...'

With a flurry of excitement, Scott started searching through Hercules' program files until he found network devices.

'Scotty boy, you are the dog's bollocks,' Scott said, mimicking Danny as he turned on the conference camera at the front of Blink Defence System's command centre.

'Just add the sound and, hello, what are we up to?' said Scott quietly, his eyes looking over the characters in the command room. 'I think I'll just.' Scott hit the record button on his laptop as he watched the camera feed.

'Good evening, General, Agent Johnson, we are all ready for you,' said Theo, watching Kyle escort the two men into the command centre.

'Mr Blazer, I have the target information here for you,' said the General, handing over a memory stick.

'Phil, would you do the honours please?' said Theo, handing the stick over.

A few seconds later, pictures and information spread across the screens.

'The target is Fahd Bin Awad, he's been funding extremist groups in the US through an American businessman who acts as the go-between to get the money into the US. Fahd has connections with the Saudi royal family, which is why we need a Saudi national with no traceable link to the US to take him out. Fahd and his contact will be at the Jewel of Nizam restaurant in Mecca at 2:00 p.m. There is a suicide vest hidden behind the bins at the rear of the building. It's set to go off at 2:00 p.m. We just need a drone to put it on and walk into the restaurant at 1:59. Their deaths will go down as revenge for a deal Fahd backed out of last month. The snub angered a local extremist group.'

'My pleasure, General. Phil, Brian, can you get me a list of drones in the local vicinity? I want exact locations, cellular access, full backgrounds,' said Theo, his confidence and arrogance returning now that he felt in control of the situation.

'I've got four, coming up now, boss. Best match is Ahmed Khan, he's twenty-three, his social says he works in a bakery a hundred yards from the target building and his phone is on and located in the bakery, so we can assume he is at work. Second best is Ali Hussain, he's nineteen and is at his home address five minutes' walk from the target, playing Command to Kill online as we speak,' said Phil, smiling smugly across the room at Brian who'd failed to get the information up quick enough to get the spotlight.

'Excellent work, Phil. General?'

'Agreed. Ahmed's first choice with Ali on backup. Time check,' the General ordered.

'Local time on screen now, General,' Brian blurted out, almost falling off his chair to get the time up before Phil.

'Ok fifteen minutes to go. Activate Ahmed.'

'Certainly, General. Phil, make the call.'

Piping the audio through the command centre's speakers, Phil dialled Ahmed's mobile.

'Hello?'

'New orders from command,' said Phil clearly.

The line went quiet for a couple of seconds.

'I'm sorry, who is this?' said Ahmed in return.

'New orders from command,' Phil repeated louder.

'I think you have the wrong number, my friend,' said Ahmed before hanging up.

'Ok, no panic. We predicted there might be a small percentage of those who complete the program that will not trigger. Move on to the backup please, Phil,' Theo said, speaking fast to calm the General before he exploded.

'Ok, I'm going to trigger him through the game. Right, we have control of his headset mic and speakers in three. One, two, three. New orders from command.'

'What the hell is this shit? Hey, whoever you are, get off my headset. That's not cool, man, interfering with a man's headset while he's playing.'

'I said new orders from command.'

'I heard you the first time, bro, now get out of my game.'

Phil looked at Theo and shrugged.

'What the hell's going on, Blazer?'

'This can't be... I, er, try the third on the list, now, hurry,' said Theo, his mind racing, the sight of the General's men taking a few steps in from the back of the room not helping his nerves.

CHAPTER 42

'The freight elevator to the loading bay is on the far side of the room,' Nicki yelled, her ears still ringing from the explosion.

'Forget the elevator. Where's the stairs?' Danny replied, grabbing her hand and pulling her through the smoke and dust until they emerged into clear air halfway into the R&D room.

'The stairs, through the fire exit,' Nicki said, pulling Danny to the left.

They got within a few feet of the door when bullets whizzed by their heads, thudding into the wall in front of them. Putting his hand in the small of Nicki's back, Danny launched her forward, slamming her into the release bar on the fire door, knocking it open as she tumbled through. Twisting, Danny went down on his side, firing back at Karl and Maaka as he slid through the open door after Nicki.

Ducking down behind the workstations, Maaka and Karl split left and right. As soon as Danny disappeared, they ran for the fire exit.

'Move, move, move!' Danny shouted, jumping down the stairs three at a time after Nicki.

When they reached the large storeroom at the bottom with the loading doors at the far end, Danny reached inside his pocket and pulled out the last explosive device. He set it to twenty seconds and hit enter before throwing it up onto the landing where the stairs turned. Ducking back into the storeroom, he ran to join Nicki on the far side as she raised the loading bay door.

'That'll do,' Danny said, dropping down to roll under the two-foot gap.

Nicki rolled under a second later, jumping at the boom of Danny's device exploding on the stairs, rattling the loading bay door behind them. Taking her hand, Danny pulled her upright. The two of them ran for the car. Danny got in the driver's seat and jammed it in reverse. He hit the gas and flew backwards before sliding the front around, crunching it into first and flooring it out of the car park. After a few turns, Danny slowed to the speed limit and blended the unremarkable looking Nissan Qashqai in amongst all the other unremarkable looking cars milling around the city.

'What the hell was I thinking taking you? That was way too close, you could have been killed,' Danny said, his face set like stone.

'Hey, it's alright, I'm fine,' Nicki said, putting her hand on his leg.

'I can't lose someone again, you should keep away from me. Everyone I get close to gets hurt.'

'Look, I'm a grown woman. I make my own choices and take my own risks, ok? I also choose who I want to be with, and I want to be with you,' Nicki said, staring at Danny while he drove.

The car descended into awkward silence. Eventually,

Danny's face softened. He shook his head, looked at Nicki and gave her a smile.

'I want to be with you, too. Now call your brother and tell him to wrap it up. We'll be there in ten minutes.'

———

Reaching the fire door ahead of Karl, Maaka caught most of the blast wave, knocking him back off his feet. Winded, he coughed and spluttered as he rolled on his front to get up.

'Arr, fucking Pearson,' Karl shouted, punching a computer monitor off the desk beside him in frustration.

'Fuck, we're going to have to call Blazer,' said Maaka, sitting down heavily into an office chair to get his breath back.

'Shit, they might be still down there,' Karl said, poking his head through the door to see the debris on the stairs.

'Nah, don't bother, they'll be long gone out of the loading bay.'

Pulling his phone out of his pocket, Maaka stared at it for a moment before making the call.

CHAPTER 43

'Mr Blazer, I've got Maaka on the line. He says it's urgent,' said Brian, in amongst the chaos of the command centre.

'Not now, Brian.'

'What the holy crap is going on, Blazer? Why are the drones not responding?' bellowed the General.

'Just hang on, General, can someone please tell me what's wrong with the drone program?'

'Boss.'

'Yes, Brian.'

'Maaka's still on line two. He says it's important.'

'Put him on,' Theo said, not thinking straight.

'Boss, Pearson and the Miller woman, we're at Blazer Games. Pearson's torn the place apart. They—'

'Hold on, Maaka. Brian, I'll take that,' Theo butted in, rushing for the nearest phone to take the call off speaker.

The General gave a nod to one of the Delta Force team, who moved swiftly in between Theo and the phone.

'Let's hear what he has to say,' he said, giving Theo a

withering stare. 'What were they doing at Blazer Games, son?'

'They were after something in the security server room. The CCTV system is destroyed, and we found a tool bag and laptop next to the open cabinet of the door entry system.'

'What on earth did they want with the door entry system?'

'Boss, I've found out why the drone program isn't working.'

'Yes, Phil,' Theo said, happy to steer the conversation away from Maaka's revelations.

'Someone copied the entire program before inserting new files, and twenty-one minutes ago Hercules posted out messages to the entire drone database.'

'Messages? What was in them?'

'I don't know. Someone deleted the contents shortly afterward. But if I had to guess, I'd say they changed the trigger command.'

'No, that can't be. How? Hercules would have detected any hack attempt and shut it down.'

'It didn't come from outside the system, boss, it came from your home link.'

'My computer in my apartment? How?' Theo stood, stunned, his brain running through how the impossible had become possible.

My palm print. They stole my palm print data.

'Maaka, was Scott Miller with the other two at Blazer Games?'

'No, boss, just Pearson and Nicki Miller.'

'He's in my apartment. Scott Miller is in my bloody apartment.'

'Agent Johnson, go to Mr Blazer's apartment with Sergeant Pace and his men. See what you can find out. I want that copy of the program back.' The General turned back to Theo, his face set in stone and eyes dark and dangerous. 'You promised me thirteen million ready-to-go assets across the globe. Right now you don't have shit. You've got twenty-four hours to get your act together before I pull the plug on this project, and recommend the FBI and counter-intelligence terminate your software contracts,' the General said, storming out of the command room.

Looking shocked and lost for words, Theo took a few minutes to process the enormity of what had happened. Suddenly springing to life, he hopped onto one of the free terminals and started typing furiously on the keyboard. Thirty seconds later Theo hit the button to terminate the link between his home computer and Hercules.

'Phil, how long will it take to get us operational?'
'Shouldn't be more than four, maybe five hours, boss.'
'Right, it's late. Who's on night shift?'
'Jeff and Bruce.'
'Ok, get them to go through all the CCTV footage up until the cameras went off at Blazer Games, and get them to check the street cams before they entered and after the CCTV went down. Do the same at my apartment, I want to know everyone who came and went, facial IDs, vehicles, everything. The rest of you wrap it up for tonight, go home and get some rest. We'll reconvene in the morning.'

'Mmm, one might say the party is over,' said Scott, looking at the connection error message on the centre screen in front of him. He pressed the button to stop recording the lost feed from the command centre conference camera, then ran the file back a bit to make sure it had recorded.

'You promised me thirteen million ready-to-go brainwashed assets across the globe. Right now you don't have shit,' came the General's voice over the laptop speakers.

'Thank you, General,' Scott said, stopping the file and unplugging his laptop from Theo's computer. He tucked his laptop and leads in his bag and headed out of the apartment. By the time he got to the foyer, Danny rolled into the car park, driving up to the door with his lights on full. Scott got in the back, barely closing the door before Danny reversed all the way back out of the apartment car park.

'Evening, children, did we have fun at the party?' Scott said, looking at their dirt and dust covered clothes.

'Let's just say we weren't the only ones invited,' said Danny, turning off the road that ran alongside the moonlit Bondi Beach, to head through sleepy suburban streets and their lack of traffic cameras and business CCTV. He stopped briefly when no one was in sight, hopping out to change the registration plates for a set in the boot before resuming their journey to the house in Woolloomooloo. No one spoke as they drove, tiredness and the adrenaline comedown dulling the mood. It was Scott who eventually broke the silence.

'You know, I've been thinking. I'm not so sure giving Simon the drone program is such a good idea.'

'Go on,' Danny said.

'Well, we don't know him, we don't trust him and what's to say he won't use the program for himself or sell it to someone who will?'

'I know, Scotty boy, it had crossed my mind. But if we

don't give it to Simon, all this will be for nothing and we'll still be in shit.'

'Maybe not, old man. I got some pretty incriminating video footage from Blazer's command room. Maybe we could give Simon that instead of the drone program.'

'How incriminating?' Nicki said, turning back to look at him.

'See for yourselves,' Scott said, pulling his laptop out.

Danny stopped the car, and they watched the drama of the command room unfold until Theo severed the connection to his home computer.

'Who were the serious-looking gentlemen with the General?' said Scott.

'He called him Master Sergeant, US Army. Special Forces, probably a Delta Force unit.'

'It's a full confession, don't you think? So what do we do?'

The car fell into silence, their faces looking grim in the laptop's light.

'It's not our problem. Let's just give the drone program to Simon and fuck off back to the UK,' Danny finally said, trying to convince himself more than Scott and Nicki.

'But how do we know our government won't use those poor people?' Nicki said, throwing the car back into silence.

'Oh, for fuck's sake.' Danny groaned, annoyed at his conscience that wouldn't let him walk away. 'How long will it take Blazer to get his program up and running again?'

'Difficult to say, I've put a few little surprises in to slow them down. Six, maybe seven hours before they fix it and manage to find out what I changed the trigger command to.'

'Theoretically, if I wanted to destroy Blazer's program for good, how would I do it?'

'Mr Blazer hosts and stores the drone program and Blink data on his own servers, located under the command centre. One would have to destroy the servers and Hercules to guarantee the destruction of the program.'

'Isn't that risky, keeping it all in one place? Doesn't he have it backed up in a cloud or something?'

'Blazer Games is so large it uses ten to fifteen server centres around the world to handle the millions of users. But Blink Defence Systems doesn't use any. The material is way too sensitive, and in the case of the drone program, totally illegal. Blazer thinks he's untouchable. The server room and the command centre are supplied by a generator if the power goes out, and both rooms are reinforced and fireproof, with an inert gas fire system that would extinguish any fire if it were to break out.'

'How the hell do you know that, Scotty boy?' said Danny, looking round at Scott.

'I may have copied the building design specifications and architectural drawings while I was waiting for you to get back,' Scott said with a smug smile.

Danny looked at his watch approaching eleven. 'Let's get back to the house. I need to look at those plans.'

CHAPTER 44

Moored up in Sydney's Rozelle Bay, Simon and Malcolm Grand sat chatting on the top deck of the millionaire's yacht, Luna. Joel Stilwell left them and wandered down to the lower deck to take a call.

'I took the liberty of pouring you another drink,' Simon said, raising a glass to Joel on his return.

'Thanks. That was Agent Johnson. He's at Blazer's apartment with the Delta Force team. It would appear your man has achieved his goal and temporarily disabled Blazer's drone system in the process.'

'Well, he is a persistent bastard, I'll give him that. I would imagine General Simmonds is a tiny bit upset about it as well,' said Simon.

'Not as upset as he's going to be when he returns to the US.'

'What will they do to him?' said Malcolm.

'I think we can all agree that none of us can afford for this to go public, what with the damage to our countries' reputations, not to mention the outrage and crimes against humanity inquests this would cause. The General will more than likely be told to go quietly with an honourable discharge and full pension, or face court martial and time in Leavenworth.'

'I'd rather you left Britain out of your damage control remarks, Joel, if you don't mind. I'm here to assist and out of respect for the special relationship between our great countries,' said Simon, with a hint of righteous smugness.

'Cut the political speech, Simon, you want that program as much as we do,' said Joel.

'For analytical purposes only, dear boy, just to make sure nobody else ever tries this technology again.'

'Of course, as does the US,' said Joel, raising his glass to Simon.

Malcolm Grand looked from Simon to Joel, not sure how much he believed either of them. But his ambition and political greed had a stronger draw than his morals. 'So when do we bring your man in?'

'I'm expecting a call any minute. According to the GPS tracker in the car we provided, they've just arrived back at the house in Woolloomooloo.'

CHAPTER 45

'So the server room goes all the way back to the rear wall of the building,' said Danny, huddled next to Scott as he studied Blink Defence's building plans on Scott's laptop.

'Yes, that's right.'

'And there is a fire escape stairwell coming down from the command centre to the server room?'

'Yes, but the doors are both steel lined with palm activated door locks.'

'Say I get in, can I just blow up the servers?' said Danny, looking doubtfully at the two explosive devices he had left from the canvas bag and the handguns with the remaining full magazines laid out on the kitchen table.

'No, dear boy, I told you, the rooms are protected by an inert gas fire system. Any explosion or rapid heat rise is detected and gas would flood the room from pipes in the ceiling. One, it would put the fire out, and two, you wouldn't be able to breathe.'

'We're screwed then. Perhaps we should just give

Simon the program and get on with our lives,' Danny said, yawning.

'And how does that sit with your conscience, Daniel?'

'Not well, Scotty boy, but I'm running out of ideas.'

'Yes, if only we had a powerful EMP device to fry all the hard drives in the building.'

'You'd need a big one, like the one they have up at the university,' said Nicki, walking into the kitchen to get a drink out of the fridge.

'I beg your pardon, sis, they have an EMP device at the university?'

'Yeah, I've seen it. I have a friend who works at the university. It's in their new quantum physics and nanoscience department. It's a big glass building off the back of the physics department.'

Danny and Scott looked at each other before turning to Nicki. 'Where's the university?' they said in unison.

'Er, I dunno, about a ten-minute drive away, just past Victoria Park.'

'How big is this thing?'

'Not too big, er, about the size of a suitcase. Why?'

'Would it fit in this bag?' Danny said, holding the large, empty, black canvas bag from the boot of the car up.

'Er, yes, I guess so. Why?' Nicki said, pressing the question.

'Because I'm going to steal it, break into Blink Defence Systems and fry Hercules and the servers.'

'Superb stuff, count me in, old man.'

'Well, if he's going, so am I,' said Nicki forcefully.

'Look, neither of you are going. It's too dangerous.'

'Oh, so you know where this EMP device is, do you?' Nicki said, frowning.

'He wouldn't know what a server looked like even if he

got into Blink,' said Scott, shutting the lid of his laptop down.

They sat in an awkward silence for a few minutes before Danny finally gave in.

'Fine, you can come, but you do exactly as I say, ok?'

'Yes, boss,' Nicki replied with a smile.

'Top man. When do you plan on doing this, tomorrow night?' said Scott, looking at his watch as it approached midnight.

'No, tonight, Scotty boy, the Delta team is out looking for us. Blazer's other men are busy at Blazer Games. Tonight is the best time for an attack. It's the last thing they'd expect and if we go in the early hours, there shouldn't be more than a handful of security guards in the building.'

'Ah, yes, of course, terrific plan, old man,' Scott said, his face dropping.

'You can always stay here, Scott.'

'No, no, I wouldn't dream of it. Just give me a minute. I have a little something I need to do first,' Scott said, taking his phone and laptop into the other room.

'We leave in half an hour.'

Danny loaded the explosive devices into his jacket pockets and slid two of the handguns into his shoulder holsters, handing Nicki the third.

'You better have this. Scott'd only blow his bollocks off.'

She took it off him, sliding it in the back of her jeans.

'Thanks,' she said, cupping his face in her hands and kissing him on the lips.

'You can help me get the EMP device and that's it. When we get to Blink, I want you to wait around the block until I call, ok?'

'But—'

'No buts, if it all kicks off badly and I don't make it out, promise me you'll drive away.'

She was about to protest again, but the look on Danny's face told her it would be useless.

'Ok, I promise.'

'Good, now whereabouts in the quantum physics building is this EMP device?'

'It's in a big metal cage in the main lab. I think he called it a Faraday cage? Something about the pulses not being able to get through and fry all the lab equipment.'

'On the subject of frying, is there any tin foil in the kitchen? I need to wrap my phone up before I set the EMP off, so I can contact you on the way out.'

'Hang on, I'll check, yep, here you are,' Nicki said, handing a roll of foil over.

'Thanks,' Danny said, tearing off a strip, folding it and putting it in his pocket. 'Shake a leg, Scotty boy, time to go.'

CHAPTER 46

Danny got Nicki to drive round the university campus twice. The place was deserted so they headed past the sports field and the physics department and its grand frontage, typical of buildings from the 1850s. They turned down an access road to the rear which led to the quantum physics and nanoscience building, stark in contrast to the main building with its grey glass and metal facade.

'Ok, you turn the car around and park it up over there in the shadows, with the engine and lights off. Anyone comes, call me,' Danny said, giving Nicki a grin as he got out the passenger door. 'You coming, Scott?'

'Absolutely, my good fellow, I'm right behind you,' Scott said with an air of excitement in his voice.

The two of them headed over to the building, running up the stairs to the entrance doors set back in the building's glass panelled walls.

'Do you want to do the honours?' Danny said, pulling a tyre wrench out of the black canvas bag and offering it to Scott.

COMMAND TO KILL

'I rather think I would,' said Scott, taking the wrench off Danny.

'Take a good swing, Scotty boy, try to hit the glass panel with the edge of the socket.'

Scott drew the wrench back with both hands, making Danny smile as he swung it at the glass in the door as if he were teeing off with a two-wood. The toughened glass shattered into crystals, staying intact as a pane for a split second before tumbling across the tiled floor inside the building.

'Nice one, Scotty,' Danny said, brushing loose crystals of glass out the way as he stepped through the door frame.

'Yes, that was really quite exhilarating,' Scott said, following him inside.

'Where are you? Er, here we go, lab one,' said Danny, searching the building plan in the foyer under the light from his phone.

The two of them walked swiftly down the corridor, turning halfway along the building to bring them outside the heavy wooden fire door to the main lab.

'Stand aside, old man, I'll take care of this,' said Scott, jamming the sharp end of the tyre wrench in between the door and frame. 'Just a sec, I've nearly got it,' he huffed, pulling the wrench backwards and forwards.

Leaning calmly around him, Danny pushed gently down on the door handle, allowing the unlocked door to swing open.

'Oh, I, er...'

'It's ok, Scott, in we go.'

The lab was large with the kind of fixed down desks with power points and gas taps you'd expect. One of the campus walkway lights outside was flooding the room with a yellow glow. The Faraday cage was easy to spot with its mesh walls, floor and ceiling. Danny entered and studied the EMP device sitting on a table in the middle of the cage. It had a large copper coil around a metal cylinder at one end with two rows of jam jar sized electrical components behind it. As he shone his phone light on it, the words 'High-Powered Ultracapacitor' lit up. A metal box sat at the back with the word Tesla and a picture of a lightning bolt on top. There was a display screen on the side. Danny pressed the power button. It burst into life with a 'Unit power 100%' message on top.

'Looks like we're in business, Scott.'

'Excellent stuff, would you mind if we get out of here now?' Scott said, his confidence fading a little.

'Yeah, here, open the bag for me,' Danny said, grabbing the two metal lifting handles protruding from the top of the device. 'Christ, it must be at least thirty kilos.' He got it off the table and bent his knees in a squat to lower it into the black canvas bag.

They managed to fit it in, even if the zip wouldn't close all the way across. Lifting the bag up, Danny managed to get the shoulder strap over his head so the bag hung behind him, resting in the crease of his back.

'Ok, let's get out of here.'

They just got out the lab door when Danny's phone buzzed in his pocket.

'Nicki?'

'Two security guards have arrived. They're heading in through the broken door.'

'Shit, er, drive around the front of the old physics building, we'll meet you there,' said Danny, hanging up before Nicki could reply.

'Trouble?'

'There always is, Scott. Let's move.'

Running down the corridor as fast as he could with the weight on his back, Danny turned left instead of the way they'd entered. They found the enclosed walkway that linked the new building to the old physics department and headed down it just as torch lights and shouts came from the corridor behind them.

'Scott, door to the right,' Danny said, trying not to raise his voice.

Running ahead of him, Scott raised the tyre iron, ready to jam it in the door frame.

'Scott!'

'Oh, yes, right,' Scott whispered, placing his hand on the door handle and pushing the unlocked door open.

They both slid inside. Danny closed the door carefully behind them. 'Gimme that,' he said, taking the tyre wrench off Scott and wedging the end under the bottom of the door.

A few seconds later, torch light flickered and danced through the glass in the door as the security guards ran down the corridor. Danny and Scott flattened themselves against the walls on either side of the door. A guard stopped outside and a beam of torchlight cut through the dark to illuminate the far side of the room. The door handle flipped down as the guard tried the door, luckily the wrench jammed under it held fast.

'This one's locked, they must have gone down towards the lecture theatre.'

Danny breathed a sigh of relief as the guard's footsteps faded away to silence. He put the heavy bag on the table and stretched his back before heading for the window overlooking the front of the physics building and the sports field. Looking up the road, he saw Nicki parked under a tree with the lights off.

'Good girl, time to go, Scott,' he said, flipping the latch on the window and sliding it up.

Scott got out first and held his arms up as Danny

handed the bag down to him, its weight causing him to stagger backwards.

'Careful, Scott, we can't afford to drop that. I haven't got a Plan B.'

'Understood, old chap, it's alright, I've got it.'

Danny took the bag back off him and the two of them scooted over to the car, putting the bag in the boot before getting in.

'That thing weighs a ton. I think I'm going to have to rethink my way into Blink. Take us back to the Holiday Inn hotel at the airport. I've got an idea.'

Nicki drove off, careful not to go over the speed limit. A few minutes later, a police car sped past them in the opposite direction. It paid them no attention, the officers in too much of a hurry to investigate the university break-in.

CHAPTER 47

'Everyone's gone for the night?' said Maaka, entering the command room at Blink Defence Systems.

'Yeah, they left about an hour ago,' said Jeff without looking around.

'What's that?' Maaka said, pointing to the CCTV still up on the main screen.

'That is the Nissan Qashqai, Pearson and Miller used to get to Blazer Games, and that looks suspiciously like the same car arriving at Mr Blazer's apartment. Here, I think it's the same car that arrives later on. It's hard to see as he keeps the headlights on full towards the camera and reverses it all the way back out.'

'Registration?'

'Not off those but we got a hit on a traffic camera that ties up with the time they left Blazer Games. They're fake, the registration belongs to a Volvo V40 owned by an art teacher in Queensland,' Jeff said, flicking the traffic cam picture up.

'Are we going or what? I need a beer and some sleep,' complained Karl, still brushing bits of dust out of his hair.

'Keep searching for it, you see that car anywhere, you call me, ok?'

'Yes, Mr Carter.'

With that, Maaka and Karl left.

'Still nothing from your boy?' said Joel Stilwell.

'It would seem not,' replied Simon, picking up his briefcase and placing it on his lap. He fetched a phone out of it and scrolled through the display. 'It looks like Mr Pearson may have gone off plan,' he continued, following the Nissan's journey with the GPS tracker from the house in Woolloomooloo to the university, then to the airport, and now heading towards Blink Defence Systems.

'Is it time to show our hand?'

'I believe it is, Joel.'

'What's going on, Simon? Joel?' said Malcolm, confusion written on his face.

'Pearson's not playing ball, it's time to send Agent Johnson and the General home,' said Joel down his phone, before hanging up and turning to look at Malcolm.

'Hey, what's going on here? This is my deal, my country. I say what goes down.'

'Absolutely, and we're most grateful to you for bringing all this to our attention, but now you are of no further use to us,' said Simon, putting his hand behind the top of the open briefcase to pull a silenced Glock 17 out. He pointed and fired with practised precision, putting a bullet in the centre of Malcolm's forehead while maintaining a look of indifference on his face.

'Time to go,' said Joel, ducking into the wheelhouse.

He reappeared a few moments later, nodding to Simon before both men headed down the gangplank.

'Absolutely,' said Simon, following Joel off Luna.

The two of them walked casually out of the marina, got into a Mercedes 4x4 and drove away. A minute later, a massive explosion ripped through the yacht, Luna, ripping its fibreglass hull into pieces before engulfing the decks and Malcolm's dead body in flames.

A knock on the hotel door woke Agent Johnson out of a deep sleep. It took him a few seconds to remember he wasn't at home with the wife and kids. 'Yeah, yeah, hang on.' When he opened the door, he was surprised to see Sergeant Pace with one of the other Delta Force soldiers on the other side.

'Agent Johnson. Agent Joel Stilwell thanks you for your assistance in this matter, but we are taking control of this mission from now on. Could you get dressed and pack your bag? Your flight back to Fort Bragg is in forty minutes.'

Johnson did as he was asked and was soon sitting in the back of a car with two Delta men up front. They drove out of Sydney, leaving the buildings and street lights behind until they reached the remote Holsworthy Military Airport. The gate was expecting them and let them through without a problem. They drove across the base, pulling up next to the rear ramp of a massive US Air Force C-17 Globemaster cargo plane.

'This way, sir, we're about to leave,' said an airman on the ramp.

As Johnson walked up the ramp, he saw the General on the bench seating that ran down either side of the cavernous space inside the plane. He was handcuffed,

STEPHEN TAYLOR

flanked either side by two hard-faced military policemen. Johnson sat down opposite the General, buckling the shoulder straps down as the hydraulic motors whined and the massive ramp closed. As the jet engines wound up to speed, Johnson sat looking passively across at the General as he stared hatefully back.

CHAPTER 48

'You stay here until I call, then come and pick us up outside of Blink, ok?' said Danny through the lowered Nissan window.

'Yeah, be careful,' Nicki said, looking up at him.

'Always am,' Danny said with a smile.

'No, I mean it. Be careful,' she said, reaching out and grabbing his t-shirt, pulling him down and kissing him through the window.

'I will,' Danny said, pulling away slowly.

'And look after my brother,' she shouted as he walked away.

Danny climbed into MacIntyre's black Audi A8 and powered the five-litre engine away.

'Are you ok about this, Scott?'

'I wouldn't have it any other way. Unfortunately when it comes to computers you are like something out of the dark ages. You need me to check the servers and Hercules are permanently wiped.'

'Yes I do, mate, is your stuff sealed?'

'I'm pretty sure it'll be ok. I've wrapped my laptop and

phone in so much kitchen foil I don't think anything will get through, including me,' Scott said, grinning.

'Ok, here we go.'

Danny pulled the car up to the barrier and lowered the window to the security guard in his hut.

'Hey, buddy, I've got an early morning limo pickup for Mr Blazer.'

'I think there's been some sort of mistake. Mr Blazer's not here.'

'No mistake, look, I've got the paperwork here,' Danny said, flashing some paper he'd found in the glove box.

'Hang on,' the guard said, begrudgingly getting up out of his warm security hut to walk to the car in the fresh early morning air.

'Here, take a look,' Danny said as the guard bent down to look into the car.

In a flash, Danny grabbed the collar of his shirt in one hand and powered his fist into the man's face repeatedly with the other. After the fourth bone-crunching punch, the guy's eyes rolled back into his head and he slid down the outside of the car to the ground.

'I really think you should address your anger issues, Daniel,' said Scott, watching Danny get out and drag the man back into the security hut.

He zip tied his hands and feet, then hit the button to raise the gate on his way out. Driving around to the rear of the building, Danny turned the car to face the outer wall of the server room. Reversing it back as far as it would go, Danny put the car in park and got out with Scott. He popped the boot open and heaved the canvas bag containing the EMP device out and put it on the floor, then reached in and grabbed the tyre iron. Scott took out his considerably lighter rucksack with his laptop and phone in and stood to one side.

'Here we go,' Danny said, moving back to the open driver's door. He stretched his foot in and pressed it firmly on the brake pedal before reaching down and clicking the car into drive. The car moved slightly as the engine tried to pull the car forward against the brakes. Balancing on one leg while keeping the brake down, Danny touched the end of the tyre wrench on the top of the accelerator pedal.

'Ok, one, two, three,' he said, pushing the accelerator pedal flat to the floor with the tyre wrench, wedging its other end into the driver's seat as he released the brake and spun out of the car. Turning his head back, Danny watched two tons of powerful Audi take off, accelerating ever faster in the short distance between them and Blink's outer wall.

'What?'

'Sorry to bother you, Mr Carter. You said to call if we had any news on the Nissan Qashqai.'

'Talk,' said Maaka, already out of bed and pulling his clothes on.

'Er, yes, sir. We had a hit on a traffic camera a couple of miles from here, so I checked all available traffic cameras the vehicle would pass on its exit from the area and came up blank. Now this is the really clever bit. I started hacking local businesses' CCTV and door cameras until I got a hit, then I—'

'Get to the point, Jeff,' Maaka growled.

'Yes, sorry. The Nissan is in a housing estate about a mile away from here, parked up on Rose Street. Do you want me to... Hello? Mr Carter? He hung up. How rude.'

'Should we let the boss know?' Bruce said, looking at his watch, not sure whether to wake Theo up or not.

'I suppose we'd better, I'll flip you for it, heads or tails?'

'Oh no, you found the Nissan. You make the call,' Bruce said, turning away from him back to his monitor.

'Shit.'

A loud boom from somewhere underneath them stopped him as he lifted the phone. The vibration could be felt through the floor, rattling the pens and coffee cups on the desk in front of him.

'Christ, what the hell was that?'

'I don't know, I'll call security,' Bruce said, hitting the extension for the security desk in the main reception.

CHAPTER 49

'In we go, Scotty boy,' said Danny, squeezing himself through the gap between the demolished wall and the impaled Audi.

Initially he couldn't see anything. A cloud of brick dust hung in the air around the impact site. Moving through it, Danny could see the server room with all its tall data cabinets full of PCs and flashing lights and whirring cooling fans. He moved swiftly to the centre of the room and put the canvas bag down to unzip it. Scott slid through the gap in the wall and joined him as he pulled the EMP device out and placed it on the floor.

'Is here a good place?' he asked Scott.

'I would say so, it's pretty much central, and Hercules is directly above us.'

'Good, can you operate it? I'm expecting company any second,' Danny said, pulling the gun out of his holster as he headed to check the entrance door.

'I'd rather you kept that kind of information to yourself,' Scott said, turning the LCD screen on and tapping through the commands.

'Let's see, choose power setting. Set to max. Engage firing sequence, yes or no? Absolutely.' Scott said, hitting the yes button, the word 'Priming' and a thirty-second counter appeared.

'Thirty seconds,' Scott shouted to Danny at the door.

Danny had an ear to the metal door. He could hear running about and a voice.

'Has anyone checked the server room?'

'No, I'll get the passkey.'

He turned back to join Scott as the clock ticked to zero. The device made a high-pitched whistling sound. At the same time, all the lights went out. Little electrical crackling sounds and sparks popped, spreading from the cabinet next to them to the far walls in a hundredth of a second, leaving Danny and Scott standing in the middle of the room in the dark until the emergency generator kicked in a few seconds later.

'Well, that was exciting,' Scott said, looking around at the smouldering servers.

'I guess you don't need to check that these are wiped.'

'I guess not. Shall we move straight on to Hercules?'

'Yep, let's go,' Danny said, unwrapping his mobile from all the kitchen foil, thankful to see it spring into life as he turned it on.

As they headed for the fire door and stairs to the command room above, they could hear shouts and hammering from the entrance door behind them.

'I imagine the EMP device has fried the electronic door locks as well.'

'Good, that'll buy us enough time to check Hercules and get out the way we came in.'

Danny took the lead, heading up the stairs to a second fire door. He darted his head across to take a mental picture of the command room beyond, no security running around and only a couple of nerds standing around looking confused. Pulling the door open, Danny swept into the room with his gun pointed at Jeff and Bruce.

'Oh shit,' said Bruce, his face dropping as he raised his hands.

'Just sit back down in your chairs and do nothing. We'll be on our way in just a minute. Is anyone else in here?' Danny said, his face hard as granite and eyes locked in their direction. Jeff and Bruce didn't need telling twice.

'No, the door lock's broken, no one can get in or out.'

Scott wandered in behind Danny and moved over to the three massive data cabinets that housed the super computer Hercules. There were some lights still on in the cabinet, so he ripped off the kitchen foil covering his laptop and connected it up to Hercules.

'Are we good, Scott?' Danny said, without taking his eyes off Bruce and Jeff.

'Just a minute, Daniel, still checking.'

'You're Scott Miller,' said Bruce enthusiastically.

'I most certainly am.'

'The Scott Miller, your security systems are the best in the world, man.'

'Why thank you, er…?'

'Bruce, Bruce Reeve.'

'Although I hate to break up the Scott Miller fan club, can we get on with this and get the fuck out of here?' said Danny, rolling his eyes.

'Oh yes, sorry, old man. Yes, Hercules is dead.'

'Good, call Nicki, tell her to come and get us. You two just sit tight until we're gone.'

Jeff and Bruce nodded agreeably and didn't move an inch as Danny and Scott backed out the fire door. Danny went ahead while Scott called Nicki. He came back into the empty server room to hear the guards battering the door with something heavy and hard as they attempted to break it down.

'Daniel, she's not answering,' Scott said, as he caught up.

'Fuck, try her again when we get outside.'

Danny squeezed back out of the gap into the car park and headed along the side of the building towards the road, with Scott followed close behind him. As they neared the front of the building, two security guards walked round the corner from reception, nearly bumping into them. Everyone stopped in surprise and looked at each other, apart from Danny, who immediately kicked one guard in the balls before side-swiping the other on the temple with the side of his gun. The men went down on the ground, one semi-conscious, the other holding his crotch in agony.

'She's still not answering,' Scott said, following Danny as he ran out the gate.

'Fuck, keep running, Scott, we'll go to her,' Danny said, picking up the pace as he crossed the road and headed towards the housing estate and the parked Nissan.

CHAPTER 50

Nicki sat in the car, nervously looking at her watch. 'Come on, come on,' she muttered.

The mobile ringing on the passenger seat beside her making her jump. Looking over, she was relieved to see Scott's number displayed on the tiny screen. As she reached across to answer it, a tap on the driver's window made her look back. Sergeant Pace had appeared out of nowhere and was tapping the barrel of his M1911 pistol on the glass. Nicki turned to grab the phone to warn Scott and Danny, but the passenger door whipped open and another one of the Delta Force team snatched it away before she could reach it. Sergeant Pace opened the driver's door and gestured for her to get out. As she did, he took the handgun from the back of her jeans and waved a signal. A set of headlights came on a hundred metres down the road, growing larger as the car accelerated, before braking hard to a stop alongside them.

Danny got to the car well ahead of Scott, pulling the door open sharply, then slamming it shut with rage and frustration at its empty interior.

'Fuck,' he shouted, banging his fist down on the car roof.

He turned to see Scott catching up to him, his bag containing his laptop and phone hanging off his shoulder as he tried to run with a stitch. A phone ringing interrupted his thoughts. Danny reached for his pocket before realising it wasn't coming from his phone. Looking into the car, he saw the light from Nicki's mobile glowing on the passenger seat. Pulling the door open, he dived across and grabbed it.

'Hello,' he said, holding a hand up to silence Scott as he reached the car.

'Daniel, my, you have been a busy boy,' came Simon's smooth, educated voice.

'Cut the crap, Simon, where's Nicki?'

'She's safe, for now.'

'What do you want?' Danny growled, his fist clenched tight on his free hand.

'You know what I want. Bring me the drone program and I'll let your little friend go. 3:00 a.m, I'll send you the address on this phone, don't be late.'

Simon hung up. The phone buzzed a second later with the address of a boatyard in Berrys Bay, across the bridge to the north of Sydney.

'Who's got her, Blazer?' Scott said, catching his breath.

'No. Simon.'

'He wants the program?'

'Yep.'

'We'll have to give it to him then,' Scott said, getting into the passenger seat.

'No, we haven't come this far just to hand it over, there must be another way,' said Danny, getting in the driver's side.

'So what do we do?'

'Mmm, perhaps we could get a little backup,' Danny said, an idea starting to formulate in his mind.

Looking in the mirror before pulling off, Danny saw Maaka's black Toyota Land Cruiser slide sideways into the street a hundred metres behind them.

'Ah, give me a fucking break. Buckle up, Scott, we've got company.'

Danny floored the accelerator and took off as fast as the mediocre 1.7 litre engine could go. They barely got out of the housing estate before the powerful Toyota closed the gap between them. The Nissan squealed onto the main road, its tyres fighting for grip as the back end snaked before the vehicle straightened up. The Toyota came out faster, sliding sideways onto the wrong side of the road before gaining grip. Karl opened the passenger window and slid his head and torso out, his gun out and steady aiming at the Nissan, trying to get a lock on the silhouette of Danny in the driving seat as it snaked down the road.

'Shit, keep down, Scott,' Danny yelled, jerking the Nissan to one side as he looked at Karl in the rear view mirror.

Two bullets punched through the rear window, shattering it into a million pieces before exiting out the middle of the front window, one shattering the mirror as it went.

'Take this, Scott,' Danny said, sliding the Glock out of his holster, flicking the safety off and handing it across. 'Breathe slow, aim between the seats at their windscreen and squeeze the shots off slowly. Ok?'

'Ok, said Scott, taking the gun, accidentally pulling the

trigger and blowing out the rear door window behind Danny's head as he turned in his seat.' Oops, sorry, old man.'

'That's ok,' Danny said, shaking his head. 'Just try to keep them occupied while I figure out how to get us out of here.'

Scott aimed out the rear window and squeezed off a few rounds at the Toyota, missing the target as both vehicles moved around erratically. Bullets thumped into the rear of their car as Karl's trained aim found its target.

'I see it, hold on, Scott,' Danny yelled, pulling the steering wheel to the left just as Karl put a round into the rear tyre.

The Nissan slid around the corner out of control, its back side bumping up the kerb and taking out a trash can while Maaka sailed past, missing the turn. Hammering the car into first gear, Danny dragged it forward, gaining speed before turning into the Sydney Bus Museum. Without stopping, he drove straight into the glass-fronted museum entrance, bursting into the hangar-like bus depot in a shower of glass and aluminium framing.

'Quick, follow me and do exactly what I say. They'll be here any second,' Danny said, leaping out of the car.

'Here,' Scott said, handing the gun up across to Danny as he caught up with him.

'Keep it, take your laptop bag and find somewhere to hide. Anyone comes near you, shoot first, think later, ok? I'll come and find you when it's over,' said Danny, pulling the other Glock out of his shoulder holster.

'But I can help.'

'Not with this, mate, now go, quickly.'

Scott reluctantly nodded and scooted off down the row of antique buses, turning to look back a moment later to find Danny had already melted away from sight. The sound of Maaka's approaching Toyota prompted him to run. Seeing an old green double-decker bus, Scott jumped through the passenger door and ran upstairs. He headed for the back and tucked himself down between the seats.

CHAPTER 51

'Gone, Kyle? What do you mean it's all gone?' said Theo, sitting up in bed.

'I'm here now, the whole lot is fried, servers, memory banks, Hercules, all destroyed by some device they brought in.'

'Oh god, does the General know, is he there, and what about his bloody hit squad?'

'No one's seen him or his men, so I guess not. What do you want me to do? Call the police about the break in?' Kyle said, walking through the broken down door to the server room.

'No, no, we can't. Er, send everyone home, remind them they are bound by confidentiality agreements and are to say nothing,' said Theo, pulling on some clothes.

'What are we going to do about the drone project and all our other contracts?'

'I don't bloody know, Kyle. Miller stole a copy of the drone program. If we can get that back, perhaps we can salvage something. Where the hell is Maaka?'

'Jeff got a lead on the car Pearson and the Millers are

using. Maaka and Karl went to check it out. I haven't heard from them since.'

'Right, good. I'll call them now. You stay there, Kyle, I'll be there as quickly as I can,' Theo said, hanging up.

Kyle looked around the destroyed server room, deep in thought.

Your days are numbered, you arrogant prick.

With no one around, he scrolled through his contacts and hit the call button.

'Yes, who is this?'

'I'm sorry to call you at such an early hour. I have some information that will be of interest to you.'

'Go on.'

CHAPTER 52

Maaka threw the Toyota in reverse and hurtled back towards the turning, before dumping it in first and screaming after the Nissan. He turned into the bus museum, braking hard to stop short of the destroyed museum entrance, the Toyota's headlights washing over the bent-up Nissan Qashqai embedded in the foyer. Maaka's mobile rang as he and Karl got out.

'Yes.'

'Maaka, where are you? Blink Defence has been compromised. Everything's gone. Pearson and Miller have the only copy of the drone program. You have to get it back at any cost. Do you hear me? At any cost,' Theo shrieked down the phone hysterically.

'I'm on it now. We have them cornered,' Maaka replied, calm and collected.

'Good, kill them, Maaka, kill them all, and get that program.'

'As good as done,' Maaka said, hanging up.

Karl shot the empty magazine out of his gun and slid

in a full one. With an unspoken understanding of the tactical approach, Karl gave a small nod to Maaka and the two men moved swiftly behind the Nissan, peeling left and right as they moved inside the large hangar-like building, lined either side by antique buses parked facing the visitors walkway down the middle. Maaka waved his hand to the left twice. Karl disappeared between two buses on the left, while Maaka moved silently off between two buses on the right.

Putting his gun down, Danny dropped to the floor in a press-up position. Lowering himself to an inch off the floor, he looked under the front of a bus towards the entrance. He watched Karl and Maaka split and disappear between the buses. Popping back up to a crouch, he picked up the gun and checked his old G-Shock watch, cursing under his breath when he realised the EMP device had fried it. Sliding the phone out of his pocket, he checked the time on that instead.

Shit, nearly two, I haven't got time for this crap.

Feeling the two explosive devices in his pocket as he put the phone away, Danny moved around the front of the bus, tucking into the gap between it and the next bus. He scanned across at the line of buses on the opposite side to him. Maaka was nowhere to be seen. Working his way to the rear of the bus, Danny stopped short and looked through the glass windows of as many buses as he could before the multiple panes of antique glass obscured his vision. He stood still for what seemed like an eternity, rigid body, only his eyes moving.

Gotcha.

...ar side, four buses along, Danny glimpsed ...ace as he bobbed up to look inside the bus beside ..., before ducking back down. His head reappeared for a couple of seconds at the front of the bus before disappearing out of sight.

Karl kept low, darting his head up occasionally to look through windows and around the front of buses as he moved forward. When he reached the open rear doors of a cream, 1950s, single-decker bus, he heard a metal tapping sound coming from inside. Stepping up, Karl stared down the sight of his gun towards the front of the bus. The doors beside him folded shut, making him jump and turn. A little explosive device looked back at him, its time clicking from ten to nine seconds. Bursting into action, Karl hurtled towards the front of the bus, firing ahead of him as he saw Danny drop out of the driver's door and disappear behind a bus. With the countdown in his head on four seconds, Karl reached the front of the bus. His plan to exit the driver's door was halted by a second explosive device stuck on the driver's door, its display clicking from two to one.

'Fucking bas—'

The explosion blew both ends of the bus out like peeled bananas. The windows of the buses on either side blew in on the side closest and out on the other in a million glass crystals as a fireball engulfed the entire bus.

Danny used the distraction of the bus explosion to its fullest, barrelling down the museum between the back of the buses and the outer wall. His head and gun locking had an accident in the trouser department,' Scott said, edging out from his hiding place.

'You and me both, mate,' Danny said, reaching under a seat to get his gun.

He went through Maaka's pockets on the way out and found the car keys to the Toyota.

CHAPTER 53

Tearing up the road, Theo braked hard to stop in front of the gate to Blink Defence Systems. He lowered the window and turned to look at the security man in the hut.

'Jesus, Kenny, you look like the bloody elephant man,' he said, recoiling at the sight of Kenny's fat swollen eyes and nose bent to one side.

'Sorry, Mr Blazer, he got the jump on me,' said Kenny, through swollen lips.

'For god's sake, go home, man,' Theo said, raising the window before speeding under the rising gate.

He parked in his place by the entrance doors, hopped out, and entered the building. Four security staff eyed him nervously from the reception desk as he approached.

'And what the hell were you all doing while my multi-million dollar computer system was being destroyed?'

The four men looked at him blankly until one opened his mouth to say something.

'Don't bother, I don't want to hear it,' Theo shouted as

he moved swiftly up the stairs towards the command centre.

He walked past a door engineer busy disconnecting the dead palm scanner and went through the overridden command centre doors. The room was empty and unusually dark and quiet, with no whining computers, monitors or the huge command wall of screens. Kyle was over in the corner, busy going through Hercules' dead data cabinets.

'Is anything salvageable?'

'No, the whole thing is fried,' Kyle said, turning to face him.

'And the servers?'

'As I said on the phone, they're all dead, hard drives wiped.'

Kyle led Theo down the fire escape stairs and into the server room. A haze of smoke and the acrid smell of fried components still hung in the air. Theo looked around, stunned, his gaze ending on the Audi A8 impaled in the wall.

'Ok, ok, we can make this work, er, we'll blame industrial espionage. The Russians, we'll blame the Russians. First thing tomorrow I want every engineer out here, whatever it costs. I want everything replaced. I can rebuild Hercules from my master files and be up and running in a couple of weeks. When Maaka gets the drone program back, we can salvage that as well,' Theo said, growing in confidence as he convinced himself he had a hold on the situation.

'Don't you think you should drop the drone program, considering the chaos it's caused?' said Kyle, frowning at Theo.

'No, I do not. We'll get the General back on side and everything will be fine. Remember your place, Kyle, if I gaffer tape over her mouth, and her hands tied and held above her on a hook dangling from a hoist mounted on the building's girders.

'Mr Pearson, so good of you to join us. For a minute there I thought you might have had other plans,' said Simon, a smug look on his face.

Sergeant Pace stepped forward and handed the hard drive to Joel before standing to one side, his gun trained on Danny's forehead.

'Cut the crap, Simon, and let Nicki go.'

'All in good time. Would you mind doing the honours?' he said, looking at Joel.

'My pleasure.'

Joel opened up a tough briefcase housing a field laptop, the sort Danny had used on operational missions. He turned it on and connected the drive.

'It's asking for a password.'

'Daniel, do tell, old chap. It's getting late, and one would really like to get going,' Simon said, still smiling.

'Let Nicki down and untie her first, then I'll give you the password.'

Nobody moved. The tension grew in the silence as Simon pondered Danny's response.

'Very well, let her down and untie her,' he said, without taking his eyes off Danny.

Over to one side, one of Sergeant Pace's men pressed the button to lower the hoist. Another unhooked her arms and untied her, ripping the gaffer tape off her mouth roughly. Nicki scowled at him before moving across to stand next to Danny.

'Now, as I said, it's getting late. The password, if you don't mind.'

'Firefly.'

Joel entered the password only to see the access denied message flash on the screen.

'What kinda game are you playing, boy? That's the wrong password.'

The Delta Force team immediately closed in, their guns held a little firmer.

'FireFly, with two capital Fs,' Danny said calmly.

Joel typed again, allowing himself a little smile as the contents of the drive opened out on the screen. The smile soon vanished as he opened up file after file, confused at the sight of Scott's meetings and work schedules.

'What the hell is this? Where's the drone program?' Joel yelled.

'It's gone, deleted, so arseholes like you two can never use it again,' said Danny, still calm.

'Well, that is a great shame. I had high hopes for you, Daniel. It would seem my predecessor's faith in you was misguided. Kill them,' Simon said, the smile gone from his face.

'Sir, there's somebody coming,' said Sergeant Pace's man on the door.

'What are you playing at, Pearson?' Simon said, heading for the door.

When he slid it open a row of people stood in a line in front of the boatshed, dozens of them with dark eyes and blank expressions, carrying phones in one hand and knives and baseball bats and other improvised weapons in the other. Behind them, more drove and ran down the approach road, filling the forecourt before standing still and staring at the opening in the door.

'If we don't walk out that door in one minute, Scott will give the command to kill, and I don't think you've got enough bullets to stop them all,' said Danny, taking Nicki's hand before turning slowly to the exit.

Simon turned back to face him, the smile suddenly returning to his face. 'Well played, Mr Pearson. Perhaps my predecessor did have the right idea about you after all.'

'The drone program has been deleted, Simon, and once we're out of here, I'll send these people home and delete the database of all the poor people who were on it.'

Danny passed him and walked out the door. He turned after a few steps. 'Oh, and if you ever come near me or my friends again, I'll kill you.'

Simon may have kept smiling as Danny and Nicki walked through the drones and up the approach road, but his eyes burned furiously as he watched them leave.

They stood trapped in the boatshed for fifteen minutes before hundreds of message beeps sounded. The crowd of drones looked blankly at their phones before turning in unison and making their way back up the approach road, disappearing into the early morning darkness.

'That's it then,' said Joel as his men wrapped everything up.

'It would appear so, until the next time,' Simon said, shaking Joel's hand.

'Until the next time.'

As Joel and the Delta Force unit left, Simon looked at his watch for UK time and got out his phone. 'Evening, Sandra, could you get me on the next flight back to the UK please, first class.'

'Of course, sir, was it a good trip?'

'I'm afraid not, my dear. But you can't win them all.'

CHAPTER 55

Theodore Blazer pulled up outside his apartment, too tired to think about the disastrous last few days. He headed up in the lift and entered his penthouse apartment through the broken door. Leaving the lights, he walked into the kitchen under the moonlight beaming in from the large sliding doors to the terrace. Placing his phone and wallet on the kitchen worktop, Theo grabbed a glass and some ice from the freezer before pouring a generous helping of a very good twenty-year-old scotch. He took a big gulp before resting his hands on the kitchen worktop and forehead on the wall cabinets as he let out a big sigh.

'Bad day, Mr Blazer?' came a heavily Russian accented voice from behind him.

Theo turned in a panic. He could just make out a silhouette of somebody sitting on his sofa.

'Who's that? What are you doing in my apartment?' Theo said, trying to summon confidence into his voice.

The light snapped on, blinding his eyes for a second, before revealing a silver-haired man with classic Russian features and piercing, sky blue eyes, sitting on his sofa. On either side of the room stood suited men, big men, with short crew cuts and thick necks, their suits straining over muscular bodies. Theo's first thought was to make a break for the door, but as he looked that way, the man next to the light switch pulled his jacket subtly to one side, shaking his head as he exposed the butt of a handgun.

'Come, sit down, finish your drink,' said the man on the sofa, a smile on his face.

Shaking slightly, Theo did as he was told.

'Good, sit, sit. You look like shit, bad day, da.'

'As a matter of fact, yes. Now, who are you and what do you want?' Theo said, his mind spinning.

'My name is Lem Vassiliev. Yes, I know. You've never heard of me, not many have. I run a very special department of, shall we say foreign affairs, for the Kremlin. I believe you know—sorry, I should say knew—one of my operatives, Natasha Shayk?' said Lem, his tone neutral, neither threatening nor friendly.

'Er, yes, terrible accident, poor girl,' Theo replied as calmly as he could, his heart beating fast in his chest as he took another gulp of his whisky.

'Come now, Mr Blazer, take credit where credit is due. Activating that van driver with your drone program to crash into Natasha at the restaurant was inspired. It's a shame the program is no more, or we would be having a totally different conversation. You should have left him alone. I know from personal experience it's a really bad idea to pick a fight with Daniel Pearson.'

'No, no, you've got this all wrong. It was General Simmonds who ordered Natasha's death. It had nothing to do with me, I promise. Look, we can work together. I did it once, I can build the program again,' Theo said, his mind racing as fast as he was speaking.

'Shh, Mr Blazer, we know exactly what happened. Mr Drago has been most helpful with filling in the details,' said Lem with a smile.

Kyle. No, it can't be. That treacherous bastard.

One of Lem's guys walked to the large glass sliding doors to the terrace and opened them. At that moment Theo noticed they were all wearing gloves. Lem got up and gestured towards the open door.

'If you don't mind, Mr Blazer.'

'What, what are you going to do with me? Look, I'm a very rich man. I can pay you more money than you can ever imagine,' Theo said as Lem's other man moved beside him and pulled him up off the sofa by the arm.

'Mr Blazer, please, die with a little dignity,' Lem said, the other man moving to Theo's side.

The two of them easily manhandled Theo out onto the terrace.

'A beautiful view, Mr Blazer.'

'No, please, you can't do this. Please,' Theo begged, tears rolling down his cheeks.

Lem's face suddenly contorted with anger as he leaned in close. 'Did Natasha have a chance to beg for her life before you ordered her death? No, I think not.' With that, he jerked his head towards the railings.

His men threw Theo over to the top, screaming all the way down until he hit the roof of his BMW with a massive boom, blowing out the windows as the roof crushed down onto the seats beneath it. The alarm wailed as he lay there, his eyes open, locked in fear, blood trickling out of his ears.

Straightening his suit jacket, Lem turned and walked out of the apartment, his two men falling in behind him as he went.

CHAPTER 56

They headed back towards Nicki's in silence. Danny drove with Nicki on the passenger side leaning across to rest her head on his shoulder. Scott sat in the back on his phone and laptop.

'That's it. They're all on their way home. I guess I should hit delete now?'

'Hang on a sec, Scott, I just need you to do one last little thing before you do,' said Danny, looking at Scott in the rear view mirror.

'Are you sure? I don't think we should mess about with this thing any more.'

'It's just one last little thing. I need you to search for a profile for me,' said Danny, turning into the suburb of Croydon.

He told Scott who he was looking for before pulling up outside Nicki's and dropping them off.

'I'm just going to get rid of the car. I'll be back in a bit,' he said, driving off.

Parking it up a mile away, Danny spent a bit of time

wiping down the interior and the door handles before chucking the keys in a hedge while walking back to Nicki's.

As he entered the house, Nicki walked up and put her arms around him, moved up on tiptoes and kissed him.

'Thanks for coming to get me.'

'I've found him,' Scott said, interrupting them.

'Let me have a look,' Danny said, moving to the laptop. 'Yeah, that's him. Send the command, Scott.'

Scott tapped out a series of orders and hit the send button. 'That's it, all gone.'

'Good, now delete the bloody lot.'

'With pleasure,' said Scott, hitting the button and watching the files disappear.

Seeing Nicki and Danny looking at each other, Scott got up and headed for the guest room. 'You kids have fun. I'm off to bed.'

Smiling, Nicki took Danny by the hand and led him down the hall to her room.

―――

As the sun crept up over the station, a motorbike cop walked into the station offices, his crash helmet and mirrored sunglasses still on.

'Hi, Mike, you on an early shift today?'

'I was mistaken, I have to amend my report,' he murmured without looking at his colleague.

'Er, ok, Mike, catch you later,' the other officer said, looking at him weirdly but continuing on his way.

Mike pulled the file containing his report of the events after he came round in the back of Nicki's Ford Ranger as it sped through downtown Sydney. He pulled it out and put it through the shredder, before replacing it with a new one under his jacket, describing Karl Sunia as the man driving that day. Next, he logged into the police system, and put Karl Sunia in as wanted for grand theft auto, believed to be armed and dangerous. Mission completed, Mike walked out of the police station and got on his bike. He removed his sunglasses and murmured, 'Level complete.' As he put the key in the ignition, it triggered the end of Scott's instructions. His pupils shrank back to normal, leaving him sitting on his bike with no memory of what had just happened or how he'd got there.

CHAPTER 57

Danny awoke with a start around midday, instantly calming when his focus fell on Nicki's sleeping face, her hair splayed out across the pillow. He leant in and kissed her, watching her eyes open slowly and a smile spread across her face.

'Morning, you,' she said.

'Afternoon,' Danny replied, looking at the bedside clock.

She ran her hand over the fresh bruises lying on top of old scars across Danny's torso before moving herself on top and kissing him. 'Is your life always guns, action and danger?'

'It has been. I don't want it to be anymore.'

'Good,' she said, smiling as she felt him stir beneath her.

A while later Danny padded around the kitchen in his underpants, making a coffee. He turned the TV on and watched the news as the kettle boiled.

'Good god man, put some clothes on. You look like

you're auditioning for Magic Mike,' said Scott, wandering into the kitchen.

'Yeah, yeah, you want one?' Danny said, chuckling.

'Yes please, Daniel. Oh, good grief, she's at it now. Can we please put some clothes on?' said Scott as Nicki entered the room in a cropped T-shirt and lacy knickers.

'Afternoon, bro,' she grinned, taking her coffee and heading back to the bedroom.

A report on the TV made Danny and Scott turn around.

"Australia's leading businessman and billionaire, Theodore Blazer, died last night after falling from the terrace of his penthouse apartment in North Bondi. Mr Blazer's death comes hours after a total system failure at Blink Defence Systems. The company declined an interview, but this statement was released by acting CEO Kyle Drago. Mr Blazer has been under an enormous amount of pressure lately and we believe he may have suffered a complete breakdown. In the early hours of last night, Mr Blazer caused significant damage to Blink Defence Systems' servers and computer systems before assaulting a guard and leaving the scene. Police say it's too early to comment on whether Mr Blazer took his own life or not. In other news, police were called out to gunfire and explosions at Sydney's Bus Museum. When they arrived, a fire was raging. Emergency services took three hours to put out the blaze. One body was recovered from the scene."

'Blazer's dead. Looks like someone cleaned up all the loose ends last night.'

'Quite, so we're not in any danger, are we?' said Scott, with a worried look.

'Nah. Now the drone program's gone we don't have anything any of them want. Simon knows no one would believe us if we tried to expose them, and it looks like Kyle

Drago's got what he wanted now Blazer's out of the equation.'

'Ok, well in that case, I'm going to call the MacIntyre people and tell them someone stole their car. Wish me luck,' Scott said, heading to the guest room.

'Good luck, mate.'

Danny headed back to Nicki's room and stuck his head around the door. She was blow-drying her hair and smiled as she caught sight of him in the mirror.

'I'm just going for a shower,' he said.

'Ok.'

'What's next, Sarge?'

'Let me see, we've got to call in on a Nichola Miller in Croydon. We've just got to inform her that her car, or what's left of her car, is in the pound. It was stolen and involved in that craziness in the city a few days ago,' said Sergeant Monroe, flicking through the paperwork.

'Man, that was one weird day. They're still after that guy, aren't they?'

'Yeah, Karl Sunia. Ex-South African special forces. They think he must have flipped and injured four people in a multi-storey car park before stealing Miss Miller's Ford Ranger and crashing into one of our motorbike patrols as he sped through the city centre. They believe he's armed and dangerous,' the Sergeant continued, showing the young constable one of the have-you-seen-this-man handout photos of Karl.

'Mean looking bastard, isn't he?'

'Certainly is. He's probably skipped the country by now and is sitting on a beach in Cape Town. Anyway, let's go and tell Miss Miller we've found her rusty tub of crap.'

CHAPTER 58

Feeling fully awake and relaxed after his shower, Danny pulled on his shorts and a t-shirt and opened the bathroom door. He took one step into the hall and stopped. The hairs on the back of his neck went up. A faint smell in the air put him on alert, a mixture of almonds, engine oil and burnt hair and skin. The almond and engine oil he recognised as the smell C-4 leaves after an explosion. The burnt hair and skin could only belong to one person. Listening, he could hear Scott still on the phone in the guest room and Nicki singing along to the radio in her bedroom. Taking a silent step back into the bathroom, he looked around for anything he could use to defend himself. He picked up the toilet brush and looked at the flimsy plastic.

Nope, come on, I need to be quick here.

Spinning a towel tightly around his wrist first, he grabbed a bottle of mouthwash and read the label—25% alcohol—before spinning the lid off. With the other hand he picked up a toothbrush and held it tight in his fist, with the pointed end sticking out between the knuckles of his index and middle fingers. Knees bent and eyes focused, he stepped silently into the hall and moved towards the kitchen. Flattening himself against the hall wall, Danny darted his head around and back again, taking a mental snapshot of the kitchen and living room. No one in sight. He took another look, longer this time. The kitchen, dining area and living room were empty. Relaxing slightly, Danny stood at the end of the hallway, listening. In his mind, he singled out the sound of fast movement above Scott's chatter and Nicki's singing. Spinning fast, he saw Karl burst from the guest room he'd used when they first arrived. One side of Karl's head was red raw with half of his short crew cut burnt off to the scalp.

The scene played out in slow motion as Danny's brain ran ahead of the movement. Karl was raising a gun towards Danny's head, rage and revenge written all over his face. Danny threw his hand forward, squeezing the mouthwash bottle as hard as he could, sending a jet of mouthwash into Karl's face and eyes. He yelled out in pain, firing rounds off wildly as the mouthwash stung his blistered, burnt skin, and blurred his vision. Pushing the gun to one side, Danny stepped in and punched blow after blow into Karl's torso, the end of the toothbrush not sharp enough to puncture skin but hard enough to make each blow excruciatingly painful.

Adrenaline and rage keeping him upright, Karl shot a hand to Danny's throat and headbutted him backwards into the kitchen. Rolling to one side, Danny scooted behind the kitchen island, grabbing something off the worktop as Karl wiped mouthwash out of his eyes.

Parking opposite Nicki's, Sergeant Monroe and his constable got out of the car and walked casually towards the front door. They jumped at the sound of gunshots, flattening themselves against the wall on either side of the door, taking their handguns out of their holsters.

'RX14 to control, officers in need of assistance. Shots fired at 23 Dickinson Avenue, Croydon.'

Sergeant Monroe moved across to the living room window, recognising Karl Sunia as he entered the kitchen in a rage, his gun raised as he searched for Danny.

Tucked behind the island, Danny unwound the towel from his arm and poured the last dregs of mouthwash into it.

'Come on, Pearson, show yourself, you English rooinek,' Karl growled, his focus returning.

Danny popped up, clicking the gas hob lighter to the towel and throwing it all at the same time. The high alcohol content of the mouthwash caught light instantly, leaving a blazing trail as it flew through the air, hitting Karl's chest. His mouthwash-soaked top and head went up in a ball of flames, just as the police officers burst through the door. Karl screamed and fired his gun wildly and he stumbled around, panicking. Making a split second judgement, both Sergeant Monroe and his constable opened fire, blowing Karl off his feet as the alcohol in the mouthwash burnt away, leaving him lying on the floor smouldering.

'Everybody stay where you are,' said the Sergeant, nervously moving his gun from Danny to Scott and Nicki as they looked down the hall.

'Officer, we haven't done anything. This is Nicki Miller's house, and the guy in the hall is her brother, Scott.

I'm a friend. We've never seen this guy before. He just broke in and tried to kill us,' said Danny loud enough for Scott and Nicki to hear, before slumping into a kitchen chair with his hands up.

'Ok, let's all calm down. Are you Nichola Miller?' Sergeant Monroe said. Nicki nodded in reply. 'Ok, can you and your brother make your way to me, take a seat next to your friend at the table and we'll get this sorted out.'

Nicki and Scott did as he asked, hearing Danny whisper, 'You've never seen him before and you don't know who he is.'

Within twenty minutes, the place was swarming with police. Five hours later, after interviews at the station, the police concluded that Karl had got Nicki's house keys when he stole her car and was looking for somewhere to hide out. A police car dropped them back at Nicki's house, passing the coroner's van with Karl's body inside on the way. The last of the police and forensics were packing up as they arrived. They went inside and stood in the kitchen, looking at the dried blood stain where Karl had been shot dead.

'Got a mop?' Danny said, matter-of-fact.

Scott and Nicki just turned and looked at him.

'What?' Danny said, shrugging.

CHAPTER 59

'Well this is it,' said Danny in the airport departure building.

'Yeah, this is it. Thank you for getting me that job,' Nicki said looking up at him.

'Don't mention it. Sydney's Greenwood Security office needed an office manager. You could always come to London with me,' Danny said, taking her hand.

'I can't. I've got the house and things to sort out here. You could always stay,' she said, smiling back.

'I wish I could. Well, I'd like to say it's been fun, but mostly it's been shit,' Danny said, chuckling.

'You'll have to come back, now it's quieter.'

'Yes I will. Soon.'

'Goodbye, sis. Remember, call me if you need anything,' Scott said, catching up to them with his two-thousand-pound Moncler Genius armoured suitcase.

'Yeah, see you, bro,' she said, giving him a hug.

Scott smiled and moved to the security gate for the first class departure lounge. Danny picked up his trusty kit bag and threw it on his back.

'See ya,' he said, giving her a hug.

She pulled away with a tear in her eye. 'Go on, go,' she said, smiling.

'Come on, dear boy, put the woman down. The champagne's getting warm,' Scott said loudly from the check-in desk.

Danny turned and walked to join Scott. When he looked back, Nicki was already walking away.

'Don't look so downhearted, old man, Chantelle here has promised to look after us in the first class lounge,' said Scott, flashing the air hostess a million-dollar smile.

'Great, have they got a beer in this lounge of yours?' Danny said, burying his feelings down deep.

ABOUT THE AUTHOR

Stephen Taylor was born in 1968 in Walthamstow, London.

I've always had a love of action thriller books, Lee Child's Jack Reacher and Vince Flynn's Mitch Rapp and Tom Wood's Victor. I also love action movies, Die Hard, Daniel Craig's Bond and Jason Statham in The Transporter and don't get me started on Guy Richie's Lock Stock or Snatch. The harder and faster the action the better, with a bit of humour thrown in to move it along.

The Danny Pearson series can be read in any order. Fans of Lee Child's Jack Reacher or Vince Flynn's Mitch Rapp and Clive Cussler or Mark Dawson novels will find these book infinitely more fun. If your expecting a Dan Brown or Ian Rankin you'll probably hate them.